The Grand Obsession

The author at age 27

The Grand Obsession

A Half Century of Hunting the Wild Turkey in Florida

P. W. Phillips

VANTAGE PRESS
New York

FIRST EDITION

Published by Vantage Press, Inc.
516 West 34th Street, New York, New York 10001

Manufactured in the United States of America
ISBN: 0-533-13854-X

Library of Congress Catalog Card No.: 00-93433

0 9 8 7 6 5 4 3 2 1

To my wife, “Miss Jessie,” who has heard too many turkey calls past ten o’clock in the evening

Contents

Foreword

Though I served as book editor for *The Tampa Tribune* for many years, I have never before recommended a manuscript to a publisher. But I believe Phil Phillips' account of his adventures in the Florida woods deserves a wide audience. Phil was a pilot for the Florida Game and Fresh Water Fish Commission for more than thirty years. He is an accomplished woodsman and devoted turkey hunter. But while his book offers a lot of useful advice for turkey hunters, this is much more than a how-to volume.

Phil vividly brings to life a still-wild Florida during a time when one could ride a train into the Cypress Swamp and get dropped off for a weeklong hunting expedition or navigate through the wilderness around the St. Johns River without encountering another person, much less a strip mall or subdivision.

Phil is a natural-born storyteller, and his folksy tales wonderfully capture the suspense, humor, frustrations, and triumphs of the hunt. These stories also reveal much about the human condition. Phil writes of friendships and life's sharp-edged lessons with wisdom and wit.

This memorable work should appeal to all those with an interest in old-time Florida and the beauty and wonders of the outdoors.

JOE GUIDRY

Acknowledgments

I would like to give special thanks to Maggie Warson and her husband Turkey Foot, for the days, months, and years that they have spent in typing and retyping and not giving up on this project even when I grew weary. They have always been there telling me that we need to get this done so the younger people who did not get to see the Florida I knew could see it through my eyes in this book. Thank you both many times.

I would like to thank my niece Betty Jane Allen for her long and hard work in making the first copy from my handwritten manuscript, bad spelling and all. I also want to thank Betty for her encouragement and faith that this book needed to be published.

I want to thank Russell Fee (former fishing editor for the *Citrus County Chronicle*) for his editing, reading, and rereading and strong encouragement; always telling me to market it, as it is a fine book. His nephew, Mr. Joe Guidry, also helped in the editing of the book with his years of experiences as book editor for the *Tampa Tribune* newspaper of Tampa, Florida. For many years, he gave me an unbelievable amount of encouragement when I needed it most. Being a turkey hunter himself he constantly reassured me the book had all it needed to instruct and entertain the reader and should be placed before people who loved this bird and hunting.

I received instruction and help in learning to read turkey sign and the use of calls from many of my kinfolks who did live and reside on the west side of the Swannee River until they departed this side of the river for a better place; although that side of the Swannee River seemed as much like paradise as I could ever want down here or above.

Cecile Sanders and his son Lamar taught me more in a few years than I could have learned by myself in twenty. They, father and son, both could hear each bird's call, and tell you what bird made it, what it meant, and why it was given. Turkey tracks, both hen and gobbler, soon became easy. Where and why they were using a certain area and how long they could be expected to use their dust mounds. From droppings, hen and gobbler were soon known by size and shape. Lamar Sanders and his father showed all of the favorite hammocks that were in continuous use by the many flocks that were there at the time I write of. They took me by the hand and we spent many hours learning how to go to each hammock, small and large, and the best way in and out without getting lost.

It's nice to marry into a family like this when you want to learn how to turkey hunt. It is worth a lot more than I can put on paper. They all lived across the Swannee River, between Old Town and Branford, Florida. I learned the use of all kinds of turkey calls from a lot of different people.

Sam Poore of Old Town, Florida and uncle by marriage taught me the use of the wing bone, probably the oldest and surely the deadliest turkey call of all types. He was a master.

Richard Wallace of Williston, Florida made and gave me a call we refer to as a scratch box today. He also taught me how to make them myself. I killed my first really big gobbler using the call he made for me. The first call I ever had was a piece of slate, four inches by three and one half by one-eighth and a fat lighter peg stuck into a corn cob. Frank Schilling gave this call to me. A finer man and a kinder lady than his wife Betty never lived. His many acts of kindness to a long number of people made living here a lot easier. No one loved the woods and streams better than Frank.

Lamar Williams of Stark, Florida gave me my first real box call. I have had three lynch calls, good ones, but I always got talked out of them. The call that Lamar sent me is the Alpha and Omega; it leaves nothing to be desired. Any call you want to make on it is there. He also gave me the first wing bone he ever made. I would fight the whole Cuban army over it, if I had to. It has pulled some very fine birds up to my blind. The good kind with ten to eleven inch beards and one and-a-half inch spurs. It must sound just like another bird.

In my lifetime I have had the good fortune to be given the privilege to hunt on land that was and is like paradise. I do most of my hunting now on a ranch in Citrus County. The land I have been privileged to hunt on belongs to Mr. Charles Strange. His kindness to me in this manner has, I am sure, and this is no loose statement, enabled me to live at least ten years longer than I would have made it otherwise. This place is like a tonic. Thank you, Charles!

There are many other names that could be added to this segment of the book but a lot of them are lost in the passage of time. When you reach your seventy-fifth birthday you begin to reach for a thought and the hickory nut rolls to the back of your head. Sometimes it takes two or three seconds, sometimes two or three minutes, sometimes two or three hours, and sometimes it stays back there until it wants to roll back forward, and that may be next week.

My son Phillip sent me a card on one occasion that stated: "Life is a ladder and we ascend it one rung at a time. If we are on the fifth rung we can not go back to the fourth nor can we skip ahead to the sixth. We must ascend each one in its own time. The real advantage lies ahead for the higher we climb the clearer the view becomes!" Wait! I thought I just saw John Quincy Adams!

I want to thank Mr. Charles Strange for the many kindnesses and privileges that he has extended to me over the many years I have hunted on his ranch. This book is filled in part with stories that took place on this ranch, a place of beauty that is uncommon even in Florida. Without this kindness I feel might have never completed this book.

I also give loving thanks to my mother, Dorothy L. Rundicky, for the encouragement and help in every way, and with the sadness that she will never read it.

The Grand Obsession

FLORIDA
GAME&FRESH WATER FISH
COMMISSION

The Ithaca Double Twelve and the Belgium Magnum

It was a short time after World War II had ended, early 1949, if I recall correctly, that I asked a few of my friends to help me find a good used L.C. Smith or Ithaca double-barrel twelve-gauge shotgun. The better grade double-barreled guns, both foreign and domestic, were priced far beyond my ability to purchase one but I knew that the Smith and the Ithaca, even in field grades, were well-made shotguns with pleasing lines and were light and well-balanced. Due to the war, guns and fishing tackle had not been manufactured for almost five years and the demand for everything was great. I knew that what I wanted would not be easy to come by but the word was out in the circle I moved in, and most of those whom I had asked knew where to look. I also continued to look.

My wait was short, about four months. One day a friend called and informed me that he had a friend who was engaged in renovating an old hotel there in St. Petersburg and that he had found an over and under twelve-gauge shotgun in the attic portion of one of the rooms and in showing it to the hotel owner, was told to take it home. The owner didn't want any kind of gun on the premises. I called the lucky fellow and asked him what he had. He told me he thought it was a Remington. I asked the condition of the gun, choke of each barrel and the grade of the gun and last but not least, the price. The fellow told me that the condition of the gun was good, no rust and the wood was good. The rest he did not know about, stating he was not a hunter and had no real interest in the hotel owner's gift other than the price he was asking. The price was fifty-dollars. Yes, fifty dollars! But remember this was 1949. I told him I would meet him at the hotel shortly after 5:00 that afternoon.

I was there with the prescribed amount at 5:15 P.M., and when this fellow began to remove the baby blanket that the gun was wrapped in I almost got the shakes. Remington MOD 32s were going for $200.00 in good condition at this period of time, if you could find one. This doesn't sound like a lot today but I was making forty-five dollars a week at the time. A used standard grade 32A sells today for $680.00 up to $1,200.00 depending upon the grade of the gun. But alas, with the unveiling of the prophet, I found that the man had a MOD 420 Savage over and under twelve gauge but choked improved cylinder and modified. I backed off. Had the gun been choked full and mod or full and full I would have given him the fifty dollars and taken the Savage, as it was in fine shape. But I wanted a turkey gun choked full and full or full and modified. I should have bought it and put it away. It brings $350.00 to $400.00 on today's market.

Later I received a call from a friend and he said a fellow named Earl Moon had a shotgun that he thought I would like and told me he would take me to Mr. Moon's shop. We met after work and drove the short distance to this fellow's workshop. Earl Moon was a most congenial man, very pleasant to converse with and easy to deal with. In a short time we had made a gun trade with just a little cash involved in the deal. I was totally pleased. I had an Ithaca side-by-side double barrel shotgun, twelve-gauge, choked full, and modified with twenty-eight-inch barrels, plain extractors, double triggers, and a fourteen-and-a-quarter inch pull with a Pachmyer recoil pad installed and weighing only seven-and-a-quarter pounds. In thinking back, I do believe that I shot this gun perhaps better than any I have ever owned. With this gun I once killed nine doves with eleven shells, which was the limit at that time.

I was shooting on an eighty-acre dove field that belonged to Lester Mickel, south of Williston, Florida. The field and the country around it was beautiful. Classic rolling hills with mature pines and live oaks. Hogs were being fattened in the field where we were shooting, and the feed planted for them were alternate rows of corn and peanuts. If you have never had the opportunity to shoot doves under the conditions I am speaking of, I can only say that you have missed one of the greatest thrills that wing shooting has to offer, if the birds are there and are using the field on a daily basis. On this shoot the doves had been feeding in this eighty-acre field for about a month and a half. I am sure that they numbered well over 3,000.

I was shooting from a stand that I picked out because a large stand of pines formed an hourglass configuration and I was shooting an opening in the stem of the hourglass. The birds were really funneling through this pass, mostly overhead in comers, and it seemed to be one of those rare days that are all too few when we just couldn't miss. I had killed eight birds when a fellow came up to me and said, "I am Marzine Hudson, Federal Wildlife Officer. I have been watching you shoot with my binoculars and I think that you have shot over the limit."

I stated that I had one more bird to put in my game bag to have the legal nine-bird limit and at that moment the bird flew through the pass and I shot and it fell at our feet. He said, "You had better break your gun open," and this I did. We began to count my birds and being a good officer he checked the area around my stand to see if I had hidden any. He then asked to see my hunting license. On examining my license, he turned to me and said, "Phil Phillips, what in hell are you doing shooting on opening day of the dove season? I have been working twenty-four hours around-the-clock. You should be out here helping me check hunters."

I told Mr. Hudson that I too had pulled some of those twenty-four hour days and that on occasion in the past a forty-eight-hour shift was not unknown to me. I also apprised him of the fact that I had breakfast that morning at 4:30 A.M. at Okeechobee, Florida, and then sprayed the northwest shoreline of the lake at Lake Port for water hyacinths before flying to my home in Williston, Florida, for the weekend. We shook hands, laughed, and after I invited him to a dove supper, began to pick and clean my doves. I was pleased that I had killed nine doves with eleven shells. I have never done this well before or since. God gave me a memory to keep for a lifetime.

I might also add that I have another very special reason to love this old gun as I killed my first three turkeys with it. The left barrel was stamped full and the right one was modified, and performance of both barrels was true to the factory stamp. On the patterning board with shot sizes from number eights to number fives, it averaged seventy-two percent in the left barrel and fifty-five percent in the right. I used three and three-quarters drams of powder and one and a quarter ounces of number six shot with three and three-quarters drams of powder in the right barrel for turkey hunting and also for ducks. This was the high brass top velocity load in two-and-three quarters-inch loads. In 1955 I used three and a quarter drams of powder and one and one-eighth ounces of number eights when shooting dove. This gun was made in 1915 or this was in information I received when I corresponded with the factory. It was as tight the day I bought it as it was the day it left the factory. I have no idea who owned this shotgun before Earl Moon but its former owner had taken very good care of it indeed.

I would like to have tried some of the new one with a half-ounce short magnum loads in it. I am sure it would have given a good account of itself but I can only surmise this. I had been given invitations to come to Copeland by Emanuel Beasly, my wife's uncle, and to bring a friend or two to hunt with me, but until the time this hunt took place, I had been unable to accept any of the many invites Emanuel had given me.

Emanuel Beasly was the chief engineer of the train that ran six days each week into an area that was owned at that time by the Lee Tidewater Cypress Company. The logging train ran north twenty-two miles back into the large cypress swamp area north of Copeland and had many spurs east and west of the main track. This tract of land was at that time an almost pristine wilderness that for the most part, other than the logging done in this small area, had been little touched by man. Large scale drainage and land development as yet had not begun. Wildlife was everywhere inside the Corkscrew area and was in abundance. We arrived at Copeland on a Friday morning at 6:00 A.M. and after having a fine breakfast with Emanuel and my wife's aunt, Dicey, we loaded all of our gear on the labor train and at 7:30 A.M. Uncle Emanuel blew the whistle on the engine and all of the logging crew comprised of eighty percent Seminole Indians and twenty percent Anglo Saxons got on board and we started rolling down the track to Spur 23, our designated hunt area. We enjoyed the whole panorama unfolding before us as we rolled northward deep into the swamp.

Here we would look and see a thousand white ibis in flight. In another direction eight deer were feeding. To the right side of the track a twelve-foot alligator lay sunning itself on a fallen palm log. Then two fine bucks were standing stark still, reading their book until they decided to take their back trail into the swamp with white flags flying. We were ready to stop at each sighting, but Spur 23 was still ahead. The mosquitoes were about as bad as I have ever encountered. I was literally covered with them and continuously fighting them off, but when I looked at the Seminole logger next to me, I saw that he had not one anywhere on him. A few were flying around his face as he dozed, eyes closed and sound asleep, but none landed. I asked Emanuel about this later and he said that the Seminoles ate a plant that made them almost immune to the swarms that were driving us wild. I tried later on in conversations with the Native Americans there at Copeland and many other times at reservations in south Florida to obtain information about the plant that worked so well for them and as to the method of its use. I was never able to obtain the information from anyone of the people I asked nor would they sell me any of the extract or give me one of the plants. This may be the last shot fired in the Seminole wars and if so, I will consider it a just retribution.

I am moved to say that a few years, perhaps as many as five, after this hunt took place a product called Off!® was placed on the market and the rest is history. With a bottle of Off! in his pack sack or pocket, white man or red brother can walk into the worse swamp in Florida and not be bedeviled. I know that a lot of people can sit in a blind and endure the constant biting of mosquitoes without slapping or scratching but I am not one of those lucky people. I know I have spooked both deer and turkey with my hand movements.

We were all brought to attention by two sharp blasts from the old time train whistle on the engine that was two cars ahead of us and the gradual slowing of the train. All at once we came to a stop and Emanuel stepped back and told us that this was Spur 23. We started to unload our gear as Emanuel told us that he would check on us each day, except Sunday. He would take our deer or turkey back each evening as the train came by and place them in the walk in cooler at Copeland. We had more than enough food to last the four days that we were to hunt. We said our good-byes and set about putting everything in its place to make a snug camp. Miles up the track we faintly heard the whistle blow twice and we knew the day's work had started for the logging crew.

After the tent was erected, the table set up, and all else seemed snug, we picked up our shotguns, and each one checked our compasses to make sure that we all knew the heading we were going to take from camp. Also we took our compass readings well away from the railroad track as we wanted no false readings caused by magnetic attraction to the compass needle. There is a lot of iron in thirty miles of railroad. With a good compass it would be very hard to get lost there because you have a thirty-mile base line running approximately north and south. But, if an overcast moved in and you had no compass you might become confused as to how to get back to the track line from the side you left on. You could wander for miles even days because the area is vast and some of it is very rough. None of us had any fears or apprehensions along these lines as we were all seasoned woodsmen, but even so, I remember reading that Daniel Boone was once asked if he had ever been lost and he replied that he had never been lost but that he had been bewildered for two or three days at a time. I had flown over the area in a light plane and in doing so I could understand very quickly the rough situation that faced a person lost or injured deep in this area. We looked around a little bit, cooked a good supper, turned in early, and we all rested very well in a snug tent.

After a good breakfast and hot coffee we each wished the other one luck and headed out to make a short hunt and to become more familiar with the country. We found it very wet going. We had packed hip boots that were just right for this type of hunting. We found a small, high, dry hammock rising out of a flat plain of water that was twenty inches deep and perhaps one-half mile wide to the next hammock. Some of the hammocks rising out of this flood plain landscape were three-quarters of a mile long by one-quarter of a mile wide and were above the waterline by three feet.

The hammocks contained cabbage palms, palmettos, ti-tis, and ferns. We each said that we would meet back at camp and have lunch no later than 1:00 P.M. Each of us came in with a hearty appetite and a story to tell of the things we had seen on the morning hunt.

We had a good lunch and took a short nap. Then we set out once more to kill deer or turkeys. I hunted hard that afternoon and as I looked at the position of the sun in the west, I knew it was time to head back to camp if I were to reach it before dark. I had been hunting on the east side of the tracks and while I had hunted hard, I had seen very little fresh turkey signs and no fresh deer signs. I finally came to the tracks at a point about one hundred and fifty yards south of the direction I was heading in. I eased on north along the tracks to the point that I had departed from and as I walked along I found one of my hunting companions, Frank Schilling, sitting beside the trail. We talked a wee bit and then headed for camp as the sun by now was getting very low.

I was in the lead and as we came to a small buck cypress pond on our right my eyes were brought to an instant focal point about sixty yards from where I stood. An object, that seemed out of place by its color and shape hung down from one of the limbs of a cypress tree in the pond. The object was squared off and from my position looked like half of a cypress roofing shingle, only it was brown. I could not get a clear view from where I was standing but I hand-motioned my companion to stand still. As I was concealed by foliage that was above my belt line, I eased down and tried to go forward to a point a little closer to the object that I believed to be a turkey. In the excitement of the moment I may have moved in a less cautious manner than I would today and in doing so I must have snapped a twig. In any event, when I looked at the limb once more, I found the object of my interest was indeed a turkey and it was standing up, darting its head in all directions. At this point I slipped the safety forward, put my finger on the back trigger, placed the ivory bead on the head of the turkey, and touched off the load of number sixes.

The swamp was so still at the moment of the shot that the report sounded like a charge of blasting powder set off in a mining shaft. The turkey tumbled end-over-end and fell into three feet of water below the cypress. I was pleased that the bottom of this pond was as hard as cement, for after a childhood of viewing films where men slowly sank from view into jungle pools, some of this must have reached my subconscious and gave me reason for pause; however, I believe I would have gone into a pool full of sharks and alligators to retrieve that bird. I was elated as I came out of the water and walked ashore with my first turkey. Douglas McArthur could surely not have felt more proud when he walked out of the ocean onto Philippine soil stating, "I have returned." The bird was a hen, perhaps two or three years old judging from the size, weight, and feathers. We dressed the bird, plucked the feathers, and put it into our ice chest.

We had a fine meal and sat around the campfire warming ourselves. I think I recall that someone had a family medication that he had brought, stating that it was to be taken each evening at campfire time. The medication was made in a heavily wooded section of Butler County in copper vats by a few trusted men who knew the recipe. It was as clear as water and had an odd taste and smell. In the beginning I didn't hold a great deal of faith in what my companion said about its power to ward off illness of all sorts and make one feel that all was right with the world but after trying it a time or two, I began to feel good about this Butler County elixir.

We sat around the fire until we were all in a restful mood, then one by one we eased into the tent after quenching the fire. We had all been into a heavy slumber when I was awakened by pots and pans flying in all directions, setting up quite a commotion. I thought one of my companions had gone out into the night for an urgent matter and had forgotten his flashlight. After a bit of rushing around, things quieted down and I rolled over and went back to sleep.

When we awakened we began to tease each other as to who got up and knocked the table over, waking everyone up. We came out of the tent, looked around, and after close observation we saw who had gotten up in the middle of the night and knocked the table over along with the pots, pans, and dishes. It was not one of us. A sow black bear and two cubs had done a fine job of scattering food and utensils from one end of Spur 23 to the other.

We did find enough to make breakfast and hot coffee. We finished our light repast, and each went his separate way. We came in at noon to find that the gentleman who had brought the Butler County elixir had shot a big buck that was using a crossing on the back part of the spur, about three hundred yards from our camp. The medicine man had set up twenty steps downwind of the trail and the buck had attempted to make his crossing at 9:45 A.M. The load of #1 buckshot that was fired hit him hard and he went down but was up and running once more as the medicine man worked furiously to clear the jammed shell in his Browning Sweet Sixteen, but knowing this fellow well and being very familiar with his temperament, I am sure he was not calling it a Sweet Sixteen at the time. As it proved to be, later on examination, the fault lay with the old-fashioned paper buckshot shells he was using and not with the Browning. Today's hunter, without gray hair, has never faced the problem of trying to force a paper shot shell into his gun that has been water soaked from being left in a damp pocket of a hunting coat to swell from the hunt made the week before. Paper shells so treated always end up being oversized, making them almost impossible to feed into the action of an automatic shotgun.

Many things are better now than they were forty years ago and shotgun shells are one of them. The real improvement began with the plastic shell. They can stay damp for a month with no change in size and they will shoot when you pull the trigger. The day of the new plastic shell had not dawned for the medicine man, so we began a three-hour search for his wounded buck. We trailed it through flat plains of water six inches deep and onto island hammocks, one after another, jutting out of the flat plains. The islands for the most part were a small quarter of an acre to ten acre of hammocks, rising two feet or so above the sheet of water. Some of the larger hammocks were quite open and once inside you could see from one end to the other. Most of the smaller ones were too tight to hunt. We did our best and we all were as the saying goes, "as good as any and better than most."

When it came to tracking, we were able to follow the buick's trail through the water, noting the portions of his trail where the water was still riled and the aquatic weeds in his path were torn from the bottom and floating. He would walk onto an island and rest there for fifteen minutes or so and then ease off on the back side as we approached the point where he had walked onto the island. Somewhere in the maze we lost his sign. After about two hours of our searching, he was able to put enough time and distance between us to make the last hour of the search as difficult as the workings of a Chinese puzzle.

The water was once again clear, looking all the same except for the uprooted underwater plants. As I stated, we hunted this buck, a fine eight-point for the better part of three hours and were never able to recover him. The weather began to change that afternoon following our search for the buck, so after a look at the weather and the forecast from the portable radio, we broke camp and took the long ride back in with Uncle Emanuel. The hunt was a good one but being younger then, I expected and was disappointed when we did not kill more game or hunt as long as we had intended. I find now that my hair is gray, I have become less interested in the weight of the game bag and more drawn to seeing what type of plants are growing in the area that I hunt and which ones are attracting the game I am hunting. Most hunters that I know who are past the age of forty find the hunting experience more fulfilling than the kill. We are thrilled by sunrises, sunsets, early morning dew on spider webs, fields of wild flowers, and the calls of birds and mammals as they greet the coming day. All of this assumes an importance to a degree not thought of when we were younger. Perhaps we just cannot see with clarity at twenty the things that are in sharp focus at fifty.

I received a card from my son Phillip in years past that stated, Life is a ladder and we climb it one rung at a time. If we are at the twentieth rung we must stand there and enjoy it because we cannot step back to the lower rung nor can we leap ahead and skip a rung or two. Each rung must be taken in its time but there is one grand advantage. The view becomes so much clearer with each rung that we climb. So ended a hunt that took place in an area that probably looked the same at the time man was first writing history on the banks of the Nile as it did when we had our encampment on Spur 23.

I would like to be able to say that I killed many, many a turkey with the Ithaca, but such was not the case. A short time after this hunt took place I read an ad in *The Shotgun News*, a publication that came out once each month with listings of thousands of shotguns, rifles, pistols, and related shooting products. The ad that caught my eye covered a half page. It depicted a fine looking Belgium made twelve-gauge, side-by-side, double-barrel shotgun. The ad stated that this gun had three-inch chambers with auto ejectors and double triggers. The price was not bad—$275.00 as I recall it—so I began to ponder. I talked to a fellow I knew in the gun trade and he was honest, or perhaps I should say he was honest to a greater degree than most gun traders I had met up to that point. I told him to order one of the Belgium beauties and in turn I was to give him my Ithaca, an Ivan Johnson single-barrel twelve-gauge, a double-barrel twelve-gauge marked Daniel Boone, and a few American dollars, which at the time I write of was the currency that people spoke of when they said, "Sound as a dollar," and there was tons of gold in Fort Knox to back it up with.

In due time this highly touted example of Belgium gun making arrived at the shop and I was told to come over and pick it up. I was looking in the rear view mirror all the way to Old Town, Florida, the point of delivery, because my rate of speed that morning exceeded the posted limit by quite a bit. The exchange of articles and folding money took place and in due time came the unveiling of the Prophet. This gun was perhaps one of the finest-looking shotguns that I had ever held in my hands. To say it was a thing of beauty was a gross understatement. On the surface there was nothing left to be desired. The barrels were dark cobalt blue with a small ivory bead at the barrels' end.

The standing breech was color-case hardened with a small amount of tasteful scroll engraving. The wood was Italian walnut with much contrast from dark to light. The beaver tail forearm matched the butt stock in color and grain. The fit of metal to wood was very good. It had a Pachmyer-type recoil pad installed and the length of pull was 14 and a quarter inches and drop at comb was two inches. All in all, I was more than pleased, or that was my feeling at the time I walked out of the door of the gun shop at Old Town, Florida. The feelings I came to have a month later were somewhat different. I had a month to wait before the hunting season opened, so this gave me ample time to pattern this gun, and I wish I could say that I did. I was unable to pattern this gun before I bought it due to the fact that it was new and sealed in the box. I did, however, have opportunities to check this treasure of the gun maker's art on two turkey hunts, the results of which I shall now relate.

Both hunts took place northwest of Old Town, Florida. I was hunting with Lamar Sanders, a relative by marriage, when I killed the first turkey with this gun. We were making an afternoon hunt and we started walking east on a sand logging road known as the St. Regis grade. It was built in the late 1940s and is still in daily use today. As a starting point we were checking an area known as Coon Ford, for if a band of turkeys came through this section of the St. Regis management area, it seemed they must stop for an hour or two to dust and loaf beneath the cabbage palms and palmetto bushes that were plentiful in that area, and then to feed across any one of the numerous hardwood acorn flats that were on both sides of the road as they worked their way toward the roosting spot of their choice.

Lamar Sanders, known to almost everyone in Dixie County as Buster, is now and was at the time I write of as good at tracking turkeys from one area to another, finding them feeding, and then guessing where they would fly up to roost as any man alive. He was able to find more deer and turkeys at the age of fifteen than most men can at the age of thirty. His father Cecil Sanders, a master woodsman and hunter, had schooled him in the ways of all wild things in this part of Florida, from childhood. Every road, every trail and, every fire line leading to each worthwhile hammock had been walked together by them both, from the time Buster's head came to a point just above his father's belt line until the time that they stood shoulder to shoulder. Buster and I walked northeast on the St. Regis grade from Coon Ford. We were tracking a drove of thirteen turkeys and they had ambled along the road to a point roughly two miles from where we had picked up their sign on the grade. We were standing where a large number of buck cypress heads were on each side of the road. A buck cypress head is a pond with a shallow bottom and many small cypress trees grow around the pond. A ten-acre pond is considered large. We began to check the sand for tracks in the road that turned off and headed into the direction of any of the ponds. We had moved along the road perhaps a quarter of a mile when Buster asked "Phil, were these tracks here when you came out of that last head?"

I stated that they were not and then he pointed to several of our boot prints that contained turkey tracks in them, smoking hot and a sure indicator that with the little remaining daylight these birds intended to fly up in this head. We were in a period of dry times so we pushed into the inside of the pool that contained dog fennel, waist to head high. We decided that Buster was to slip to the east end of this pond and I was to remain at the entrance of the pond and watch for developments that as it turned out were not long in coming.

Buster had been gone about five minutes when I heard the first shot. I looked to the east side of the pond and flying directly to me was one turkey about fifty feet in the air. I waited a moment, then placed my barrel under the bird and then brought it back till it blotted out the turkey, then I pulled the trigger, and at this point the bird began to tumble to the floor of the pond. I ran to the point where I observed its fall into the dog fennel. I was searching for this bird when I saw Buster walking toward me and when he reached a point forty yards from me that which was lost was found. The bird was a hen with a broken wing and leg. She was not to be counted out of the race at this point. When I had an open field of fire, I shot once more and the bird was dead. I found that in dressing this bird there were perhaps twenty number six shots. A precious few for two barrels marked full and full three-inch Magnum at moderate and close ranges. I made one more hunt with this Belgium beauty and I shall relate it now.

I drove to a section of the St. Regis management area that contained one of my favorite hunting spots. If a turkey was anywhere near this place, it would feel compelled to dust, loaf, feed or just walk this dirt trail south to a spot named "Pleasant Grove Cemetery." It was a fine winter afternoon; a wee bit of a chill in the air but just right for hunting. I had taken a long stroll in my hunt for enough signs to set my blind by but as always I found it, all made the day before and in the morning at that. This flock could be in Mound Hammock, Coon Ford, or any one of the acorn flats that lay between. I was not really upset but I was a little despondent. I knew, however, that one of the several flocks that used this area might get a rambling urge to walk the Pleasant Grove road, to say nothing of old gobblers and singles that were never far away from the three-mile triangle of land.

I sat down with my back to a fine old oak, got out my slate and peg, and gave a loud cluck or two then gave a ten-note lost call. I thought that I heard an answer but then decided it was a crow or a piliated woodpecker off in the distance. I sat down and pulled out my tobacco and pipe. I began to load my pipe with the tobacco when I looked up and to my right at eighty yards stood a young gobbler. I let my pipe slip from my mouth and eased the pouch down to my side on the ground. I don't think that I spilled more than half of the tobacco in the pouch. I eased the safety catch to the fire position and with my right hand I scratched in the leaves with my fingers. When I did this the gobbler began to walk with measured tread in my direction once more. "He came," as the old timers in Florida used to say, "as straight as a martin to his gourd." In the old days gourds were home grown. Home grown, each gourd with a two-inch hole bored in it was hung by wire from a tobacco stick nailed to a buck cypress pole so the purple martins that came every year could nest and raise their young. When he had reached a point of forty yards from my position, I raised this three-inch magnum cannon, put the ivory bead on his head, and squeezed the back trigger. The action that took place from this point was far from the sequence of events I had expected. The turkey, instead of beating the earth with his wings in his last efforts to fly, had not even fallen down. He was, however, wounded and dragging a broken wing. His injuries in no way prevented his fast retreat along the east side of the small flat I was seated on. The action taking place was no turkey trot but rather more like the Kentucky Derby, and he was definitely many lengths ahead in this race. I jumped up and ran after him, hoping to use the right barrel. We reached a point in this chase where he came back out of the rough into the Pleasant Grove trail once more and began to run south in the direction of the cemetery. We both reached a point in the trail that opened up enough to afford me a good forty-yard shot at this Joe Namath of the feathered kingdom. I shoved my heels in the sand and shot, this time with the expected results. He was a fine thirteen-pound gobbler. When I dressed this bird, I found once more that the number of pellets that had struck him from both barrels was hardly what would have been expected from one barrel in a good full choke gun.

The 25-20

The first time that I ever saw the rifle I was impressed with its small size and light weight. It seemed, all in all, to be the perfect woods rifle for a fellow who wanted to travel light. It only weighed four and one-half pounds and had an eighteen-and-a-half-inch barrel. The rifle being shown to me was a Remington Model 25R, pump action carbine, in caliber 25-20 Winchester. The man showing me the rifle was perhaps the best all-around naturalist, woodsman, hunter, and marksman that I have ever known. His knowledge of trees, plants, and animal habits, along with his tracking ability was awe inspiring even to other experienced woodsmen. The rifle was manufactured from 1925 to 1936, and he had acquired this one when he was about eighteen years of age and at a period of time, in the state of Florida, when there was a lot more game than there were people.

He hunted the Florida Everglades in the 1930s and 1940s, which is to say that he had wild hog, deer, turkey, ducks, and small game in unlimited quantities and in an area so vast that unless he chose to, he never saw another person, with the exception of the few men he hunted with. In any hunting camp, at the period of time I write of, there was always one or two men who fell heir to the task of filling the game bags of the older men who were not able to hunt as hard or did not have the ability of some of the other hunters. This task is not unheard of even in today's hunting camps. The man I speak of, being the rifleman and woodsman that he was, had his work cut out for him each season in this respect. I have not named this man because times have change and some people, with today's scarcity of game and our new attitudes, might call him a game hog. He was no game hog. He loved nature too much to be tarred by that brush, but he liked to see a full larder, with everyone sharing in its bounty. He hunted in a period of time that game laws simply did not exist for most of the natives of that section of Florida.

Many of the old time Florida "crackers," if they knew a law existed, believed that game laws did not pertain to them. "Trespass" was almost a term unknown, as all of Florida at that time was open range, so as the old timers were wont to say, "Let the hide go with the hair." When it came to game laws, I guess it would suffice to say that not many people lived at the foot of the cross at this period of time. But the only thing that remains constant is change and at the time that I knew this man, he had almost quit hunting. The little bit that he did was control hunting of wild hogs that were destroying roads and pastures on a large track of land that he was hired to look after. When the hogs became destructive, he attended to these matters with a Remington .22 LR automatic rifle, and believe me, he could shoot it.

I recall riding with him late one evening and as we rounded a bend in the trail we were on, five hogs ran out of a small flag pond and this man stopped, jumped out of the jeep, and killed all five hogs, which by this time were running flat out. At the time this took place, he was fifty years of age and this would have been no easy task with a .22-caliber rifle, open iron sights, and in failing light for a young man with perfect eyesight. He made it look very easy. He gave me a hog to take home for Christmas pork, as well as a hog for each of the men that were working with me.

Christmas dinner was never better! But to get back to the 25-20. I put the rifle to my shoulder and pumped it a time or two. It felt good. As I handed it back to him, he asked me if I would like to buy it, and I asked his price. He said, "Thirty dollars," and with that the deal was closed. At the time I bought this rifle, I did not deer hunt and would not have chosen it for a deer rifle. Due to what I had been told and what I had read about the caliber, it was underpowered for deer. I wanted it for turkey and hogs, and it had power enough for both or so I believed at the time. The fact that its former owner had killed a tobacco barn full of deer, hogs, and turkey with it led me to believe it would be just what I needed.

I had only been in possession of the rifle for a month or two when the first opportunity came along to find out just how good my turkey rifle really was. It was a fine fall day and the fellow I was working with at the time was almost in a fever to go on a turkey hunt. He had sat around campfires and listened to all of the turkey-hunting stories being told each night and he had reached a point that if the hunting season had not started a short time before, he might have broken the law or tried to. Everyday he had asked me if I would take him, and this afternoon we had all of our work caught up and were really just devil dragging around camp, so I made a phone call and received permission to make a hunt on a tract of land that had some of the best hunting in the state; some deer, many hogs, and turkeys in abundance. The only drawback I could see was that I had only a description of the lay of land, and that was given on the telephone. I had rode through the part we were to hunt but that was two years past. But we got ready, I picked up my rifle, shells, and small daypack that contained my turkey call, a bottle of six-to-twelve insect repellent, compass, matches, knife, folding saw, and nylon rope and headed for the truck. The fellow I was working with, whom we will call Jack, while he was a fine wing shot, he had never killed a turkey or been on a turkey hunt. He was a fair woodsman. Having been raised on a farm in Georgia, he could read signs very well after he was shown what to look for.

As we rode to the ranch, I laid out the details of the hunt. We would travel along a dirt road running east until it came to a creek that ran north and south through the property. At that point where our road ended, the creek forked and formed an island several miles long and perhaps two and a half miles wide. Inside the island and north of the road, we entered upon a big cypress slough that was dry at the time this hunt took place, and north of this slough there were four small, high hammocks, perhaps thirty acres to each hammock and one-quarter of a mile separating each hammock. North of the four small ones lay a very large hammock of about eighty acres. All of the hammocks were high and dry.

When we parked the truck, Jack unrolled the blanket his gun was wrapped in and when I saw the gun he had brought, I almost fell out of the truck. It was a clip fed, .22-caliber rifle; a bolt action. I didn't want to embarrass him, but I did question him about his choice of gun for this type of hunt. He stated that being away from home, he had to borrow this rifle and he was much like the lady who said her husband wasn't exactly what she had wanted, but was all she could get at the time. We walked to the point where the creek made the fork, and I told him he could hunt the west side of the creek, going north, or if he wished he could cross the creek and hunt the east side. He chose to go east and I told him that if he should come up on one of the five or six flocks of turkeys that were known to use this area, he should try to kill one and scatter the rest. I told him immediately after firing the first shot, to look at his watch, wait exactly five minutes, and fire another shot and I would know that it was he who had fired and I would come to him knowing that he had turkeys scattered. We would build a blind and I would endeavor to yelp up some of the scattered flock. If he heard me shoot, the same rule applied. As we parted I noted that there was ample turkey signs in both directions. Turkey scratchings, droppings, dusting mounds in the dry places, and preened feathers were everywhere —enough to gladden the heart of any turkey hunter.

It was 1:30 P.M. when we checked our compasses and said we would meet at this spot one hour before dark. We parted with high hopes that we would surely get into a flock early in the afternoon. We had made a vow to let the deer and hogs go and just hunt turkeys. We also had no intentions of trying to roost any of the turkeys that used this creek run and the hammocks that joined it, as we wanted to be on the way out before flying up time and before dark overtook us. It was a big tract of land and never having hunted it before, I felt that discretion was the better part of valor in this case. I'm hard to turn around in the woods when the sun is out, but without a good map or a sure knowledge of how the land laid, a fellow can get turned around sometimes, and on this hunt, I had neither.

I headed along the northwest fork of the little stream until I came to a place where the stream narrowed and the bed was only six inches or so below the surface. I could see on both sides of the stream that turkeys, deer, hogs, and other small game were using this point as a crossing. Tracks were everywhere. I looked at my compass one more time, and followed the tracks across the ford. After leaving the ford, I went along the trail until I reached the first small hammock and there I found where a lone gobbler had roosted in a live oak tree. It must have been a favorite roosting spot for him, as he had a pile of droppings under one limb that a show dog couldn't jump over. I eased along and saw no birds. As I came to the end of this first hammock, the land elevation dropped off perhaps two and a half feet lower, with an old fire trail running through it that connected it to the next hammock, three-quarters of a mile north. As I walked toward this hammock I could see that a flock of turkeys were somewhere just ahead of me. I could see the imprint of many feet in the mud and taking a short look at the sign, I thought that the flock was comprised of about thirteen head of turkeys. In the wet places, water was still seeping back into the tracks and in dry sections of the trail, blades of grass with wet sand on them that had been mashed down were springing back up as I watched them. I knew this flock was just ahead.

In the very low places of this trail, an inch or two of water covered the surface, and this water was still muddy, not having time to settle out and clear again since the passage of the flock. I have observed the scene described above many times and in many places in the past forty years but it never fails to start my heart to pounding. When you see this type of sign in the trail ahead, you can get your rifle or shotgun ready because as the old saying goes, "Business is about to pick up." As I continued to ease along the trail and at each bend and turn along the way, I fully expected to see the flock that I knew was just ahead. Many times when you are this close to turkeys, you will be able to tell something of the distance between you and the flock by hearing the conversational yelps, purring, and chucks that they give while feeding and walking along. The fact that I could hear nothing ahead of me made me believe that this flock was moving faster than I had realized to reach the place they had in mind. As always in a situation like this, I had to fight the urge to hurry. Many hunts are spoiled by speed. I believe all of us who have hunted more than a few years have run off or spooked game when we were hurrying to that perfect spot where we were going to kill a big buck or set up the blind to bag the best gobbler ever seen.

One of the best hunters I have ever known, Rex Land of Umatilla, Florida, friend and hunting companion for thirty years, has a saying that makes more sense to me with each passing year. Rex has always said that when you are in game country, the hunt should start when you step out of the car and close the door. But to get on with the story. . . . I continued to ease along the trail and in rounding a bend, I could see the next hammock ahead of me. I eased on up to the edge of it and looked inside then entered into the hammock. As soon as I was inside it seemed ten degrees cooler. The dense canopy of live oaks and cabbage palms formed a perfect shade. Palmettos and wild ferns covered much of the floor of the hammock but there were many open patches also.

It was a movement in one of the opened patches forty yards away that caught my eye. I was leaning against a water oak and as I very slowly turned my head, I could see three young gobblers and feeding with them I could see six hens. I watched the feeding in progress for perhaps four minutes in hopes that a larger gobbler was there with the jakes, when one of the young gobblers, for reasons known only to himself, jumped up on a small pine tree that had fallen in some past storm. Standing there he seemed to like this ten-inch elevation that was an aid to him in looking the area over. I was standing very still and dressed in drab clothing; camouflage clothing at that time had not become the almost universal uniform that it is today. I didn't feel that this turkey had seen me until he looked right at me then looked away. This action on his part produced an action on my part, that of bringing the little 25-20 to my shoulder, lining the sights on his wing butt, and touching off the load. He fell off of the log and began to fan the earth with his wings, bouncing and fluttering on the ground in front of the log.

At his last efforts to fly—really only a dying reflex—two of the other gobblers jumped on him and both began to flog him soundly. They continued to do so until he was still, paying not one bit of attention to the shot that I had just fired nor to the frantic pumping and jiggling that was in progress behind the water oak, but more of this later. . . . The rest of the flock began to mill around and I believe that they were all about to run off together, and not being scattered, they would leave us with very little chance of getting another bird. At this point one of the hens gave a loud chuck followed by several sharp cuts and the rest of the flock took wing, and in departing the area, flew to all points of the compass, well-scattered.

I looked at my watch and what seemed like thirty minutes had really only taken three. I waited two more minutes and fired my rifle. My hunting companion, I was to learn later, had gotten turned around a wee bit and on hearing my two shots was much relived, as he was able with little difficulty to course the direction of the point where I had flushed the turkeys. Because of the fact that he had wandered farther than he had intended, it took him more time to reach me than I had hoped it would. A good thirty minutes had elapsed since my last shot and I had turkeys yelping from all directions and they had been yelping for the past ten minutes.

Near the point where the birds were flushed, I had built a good blind of palmetto fronds and had draped them with Spanish moss, and when I stopped and looked at it pleased me. All I needed now was for Jack to get there before the birds reassembled and ran off together. I was testing the visibility from the blind and rearranging parts of it to make it more to my liking, when I heard a quail calling. It called repeatedly until I realized that it was my companion doing the whistling in an effort to locate me. I whistled back, giving him my location and he traveled the final fifty yards to the blind. I urged him in and reached into my pack and took out my turkey call.

The call was a homemade one, as most of the best ones were at that time. This call was very simple in use and construction. I had taken a hen turkey wing bone and shoved it into a four-foot section of rubber tubing that made for a snug fit and at the other end, I had connected the tubing to a small cow horn. When you are seated in a blind, the cow horn rests on the ground and the wing bone is placed between your lips and sucked, producing good clucks and yelps. At this point I heard a turkey give a lost call, that is referred to today as a Kee Kee run, with a few yelps at the end of the call. When it stopped calling, I cut loose on the wing bone with two clucks and had an immediate answer in response to my calling. The bird that was calling was only forty-five yards away and off to the right of our blind. It stood there, concealed by a large patch of palmettos, yelping with every breath it took. I put the wing bone to my lips again and gave two soft clucks.

It has always amazed me that a turkey, or flock of turkeys for that matter, can seem to appear without a sound, almost as though they rise from the earth like fox-fire. You look away for a second and when you look back, there they stand and so it was with this one. At my two clucks, this bird hushed and we both continued to look at the point about forty-five yards to the right of our blind. Other turkeys were yelping all around us now. I started to put the wing bone to my lips again, when off to my left there stood a young gobbler about thirty yards away. Neither my hunting companion or myself had seen the bird move to this position, and the bird was standing in a wide-open spot looking hard for the turkey that it had just been talking with, but now could not find. I looked at Jack and although I could not speak, I formed the words, "There is your turkey," and at the same time my hand began to point slowly to the direction where the turkey was standing.

When my companion looked at me and finally understood the message I was trying so hard to convey, he became extremely excited and began to whisper, "Where is the turkey?" While this was a logical question to ask at the time, the manner in which it was asked left much to be desired. I thought perhaps Jack had learned to whisper in a country sawmill. The turkey, by this time, was hearing everything that I was, and showed signs of being ready to leave us. I started to reach over and take this fellow's rifle and shoot the turkey before it ran or flew away. I had unloaded my rifle because I had my turkey and I wanted him to kill a bird, which would be his first.

As I recount this now, it sounds unbelievable and it is amusing, but at the time, the situation was somewhat intense. My hunting partner had done everything but stand up in the blind and look for the turkey and from the expression on his face I could see that he was excited and becoming as "wild as a peach orchard boar." At this point the young gobbler took wing and when he cleared a huge old live oak east of our blind, he really lit a shuck and headed for parts known only to him.

We stayed in the blind and although I yelped and clucked from time to time, I had only one more answer and no other bird came to our calling. I concluded that the flock had reached an open flat somewhere beyond our vision and hearing, and after reassembling, had gone on their merry way to one of the other hammocks to resume feeding and then fly up to roost. I looked over to my hunting companion and he looked like a whipped puppy. He sensed, as I did, that the game was over for that day, unless we were fortunate enough to run into another flock of turkeys on the way back to the truck. This, however, was not to be. So we headed back to the truck with one bird.

Jack was all questions as to what happened and why the birds would not come to our calling after the young gobbler had flown. I explained that the birds had been flushed quite a while before he made it to the blind and that I felt sure that most of them had gotten together before he came to the blind. I offered him the bird but he declined the offer. So we packed up and headed to our homes for the weekend.

This was the only hunt that I made with this little rifle. It had killed a box car load of game from the time it was bought in the late 1920s till the 1960s. I guess the hunt I write of was the last one it went on, and the turkey I shot on this hunt was the last head of game killed with it. The bolt facing was worn to a degree that the slide had to be jiggled as well as pumped at the same time to get each shell to ride into place. I tried to get parts to restore this gun to a usable state but was unable to do so. I let a friend of mine, a gun smith, have it for parts. So like a heart transplant, perhaps it still lives on in another body. I'd like to think so. So ended the long and very useful life of a little rifle that was made in an era and used in a Florida that only a few people really know and remember, a wild Florida with game in abundance, a Florida that a man could saddle a horse and ride three days in a straight line and not see a fence or another person.

But it isn't good to dwell long on thoughts like this, not if you really love the Florida that I knew forty years ago. A lot of the land that this hunt took place on is now changed. Drainage made much of the area attractive to developers and farmers, as it always must. So we have left our footprints and little parts of our heart scattered throughout hammocks and creek beds in areas such as the one in this story. We must now be content with yellowed photographs and memories of a sweeter and gentler time. As I said before, it isn't good to dwell long on the past; the present age gives us enough to find dissatisfaction with, without borrowing on what we have lost and can never regain.

The .22 Hornet

One day in the mid-1950s, I walked into Mr. J. W. Weinmiller's Gun Shop and Hardware Store in Williston, Florida, which was also the town that I resided in from 1952 til 1973. In the twenty-one years that I lived there, I walked into Mr. Weinmiller's Gun Shop many times. More times than I should have I might add, as my frequent trips there kept my billfold in a very deflated condition. The day I speak of was no exception. I was hardly inside the store when I spotted this rifle with a bird's eye maple stock, perfect bird's eye maple and in a configuration referred to today as classic. I could see that the hole in the barrel was small. The action was small too, and it was scope mounted.

Mr. Weinmiller was talking with another customer and the longer he talked, the higher became the pitch of my excitement. If you have never been into gun trading, you may not understand this but if you have been down this path, you know exactly whereof I speak. In due time the other fellow made his purchase and Mr. Weinmiller stepped over to me and said, "Phil, you told me that you were looking for a good, used Winchester Model Seventy, in 22 Hornet and while I haven't found a Model Seventy, I traded a man out of this little Sako Hornet this week and you may find it to be of interest."

It goes without saying, that the gun was almost sold at this point, before it was ever placed in my hands. Once it was placed in them, I didn't want to let it go. I did not know as much about rifles at this time as I came to know later on but I knew enough at this point to know that this rifle, as far as beauty, style, weight, fit of metal to wood, and the way it fit me when I put it to my shoulder left little to be desired. I tried the trigger and it was perfection, about three pounds with no creep or drag. It had a Weaver KV 3X5 scope and with scope mounted it only weighed right at seven pounds, scope, mounts, rifle, and all.

As I recall the transaction, I took the little rifle away with a thirty-five dollar downpayment and a promise to bring $100.00 more. I was well pleased at the time. This was one of the first rifles Sako had imported into the United States market and they had left no stone unturned in making sure that any rifleman who picked up this little jewel would fall in love with it, and all who saw it did. I was not into handloading yet, so I bought three boxes of 45GR Hornet ammunition and waited for a good cool morning to put this doll on the sand bags and see what it would do. I had made many targets: conventional bull's eyes and a number of cardboard turkeys, life-sized and with side views. I have neglected to state that I purchased this rifle for the expressed purpose of turkey hunting but such was the case.

In the early 1950s I bought the fine book *The American Wild Turkey,* written by Henry E. Davis, and after reading it a number of times, his reflections on the experiences with the 22 Hornet in hunting wild turkeys convinced me that I had to have a high-quality rifle in 22-Hornet caliber. I was certain that I had found all that I would ever need in a turkey rifle as I looked down at the piece resting on the sand bags on the hood of my automobile. I set up targets at 100 yards as Mr. Weinmiller had advised me that the rifle was zeroed in at that range by the previous owner. I put up a turkey silhouette at sixty yards, one at 100 yards, and one of the bull's eye targets at the 100-yard range also. I wiped the bore clean of oil and replaced the bolt. I loaded five rounds of 45GR Hornet into the magazine, I stretched out along the hood of my auto, wiggling around until I had the rifle and sand bags just so. I took a deep breath, held it and squeezed one off at the bull's eye. I repeated this three minutes later and after another three minutes once more. When I reached the target, I was more than pleased. All three shots could be covered with a nickel but were high and to the right of the bull's eye. I had been verbally instructed by Mr. Weinmiller at the store and also had written instructions so I was all set when it came to making the adjustments I needed to bring this marvel of the gunmaker's art to taw. After six tries, I did.

Is there any thrill outside of courtship that can compare with that first shot that goes dead center in the bull's eye after you have made all of the right adjustments? After many years and rifles of all types, the dead center hit still excites me, and ownership of a rifle that does this each time, if the shooter does his part, is a wellspring of great pride. Owning such a rifle might even lead a fellow to brag a bit or as my good friend Frank Schilling is wont to say, "Them that can brag without lying, let them brag." He even has a forty-year-old sign to that effect that hangs in his bicycle shop in Lynn Haven, Florida with the above statement in bold letters.

After a number of rounds at the conventional targets, I then turned my interest to the turkey silhouette. This target had no marks or bull's eyes on it so the shooter had to pick the area of the wing butts as close as he could, judge its position, and make his shot. I made a three-shot group, cooling the barrel five minutes between each shot.

I was elated when I walked up to the turkey. All three shots could be covered with a dime and two of them were almost touching. I was more than pleased. I was sure at this point, that I had found the answer to the 125-yard turkey.

We have all experienced the frustration of calling to this bird that stands in an opening well out of shotgun range and gobbles again and again in response to our calling, then after twenty minutes of this sort of treatment, turns tail and walks off across the field to the woods on the other side. The turkey that flies up to roost at 100 yards is also a candidate for a rifle in the hornet class. I know many hunters will make the statement that in this case you should come back the next morning and yelp the bird to you. I might agree with this in most instances, but quite often other factors enter into the hunt that can more than justify the use of the small rifle in turkey hunting, and I will relate an experience that I feel makes my point.

I was hunting in an area along the Swannee River, north of Old Town, Florida, on the west side of the river. I scattered a drove of turkeys very late in the afternoon. Now, if I had not scattered the flock at the time I did, they would have flown up to roost within another hour. I was yelping with a slate and cedar peg striker, and within fifteen minutes of the flushing of this flock, turkeys began to call all around me. This bunch really wanted to get together. Scattered this late in the afternoon, I have found that as often as not, turkeys will fly up, give a few yelps and then remain silent, answering no call, no matter how good the caller. They are very easy to yelp up the next morning, or I have found it so most of the time.

This flock was different. I had birds answering my calling from all points around me on my side of the river.

I had hastened to cut a few palmetto fronds and dog fennels and erected a blind of sorts in front of me with my back to a small cypress tree. I kept calling with yelps and clucks. I received answers to my calling each time and could hear turkeys flying and changing limbs. After twenty minutes or so I heard a turkey flying from a distance, and since the evening was windless and quiet, I could tell that the bird was flying in my direction. In a second or two, a young gobbler flew onto a limb in a cypress tree ninety yards to my left and in landing there he began to turn his head in all directions in effort to see the turkey that had just beseeched him to join it. Although my hair was black then and is white now, I can close my eyes and picture all of this as though it happened yesterday. Memory is a strange thing; I find it hard to remember what I did last week and yet I can remember this with perfect clarity.

The last rays of a winter sunset were shinning on the tops of the trees. The gobbler, and the limb he was standing on, festooned with Spanish moss, was bathed in burnished gold. He soon gave up his search and settled down for his evening nap. I eased myself around the tree to face a little more north and rested my left hand holding the forearm of the rifle against the side of the cypress. Then I settled the crosshairs at the point that I believe to be the approximate position of the apex of his pulley bone and started to squeeze the trigger. At the crack of the rifle the gobbler tumbled end over end in his last flight. I ejected the spent cartridge, placed it in my pocket and shoved the bolt forward, chambering a new round and headed for my bird. On this hunt my shotgun would have been of little use. The young gobbler was as close as he intended to come that evening, as were the rest of this flock. They had settled in for the night and no amount of calling would move them. The fact that I would be on my way home that night, in order to attend an official function the next day, left me with no possible way to hunt this flock again for a period of over a week. Had I taken only my shotgun that afternoon, I would have had to buy a turkey for our Christmas dinner.

Anyone who has hunted turkeys for any length of time will come to know that a shotgun will put a lot more birds on the Christmas platter than the rifle will but there are times when the rifle has its gifts. A scope-sighted rifle is out of the running on a flying turkey at any range, but with an iron-sighted rifle in the hands of an exceptional shot, it can be brought off, but don't bet any money on the shooter. The gun used in the hunt I have just related was not the light, fast handling, well-balanced little Sako Hornet that had gone home with me but a rifle of a different make and different caliber, but more of this gun in another chapter.

I shot the Sako Hornet a lot that afternoon on the sand bags, and it pleased me in every way. I extended the range to 150 yards on the turkey target and was completely sold on the rifle and the results it produced. I then tested it at twenty yards, thirty yards, forty yards, sixty yards, and eighty yards. I found it to be highly accurate at all ranges. I shot a number of crows with it at ranges out to 150 yards and if I missed one it was my fault. If I wanted to show off, I would sometimes tack up the five of hearts from an old deck of cards at 100 yards and shoot the center heart. I was young and brash and for about six months it seemed that my little rifle and I were invincible among the fellows within my little circle, but as the saying goes, "All good things must come to an end," or perhaps better yet, "Pride goeth before a fall."

Somewhere down the road about nine months after this love affair started, like many romances, it began to go sour. I started shooting at the heart on a playing card and was sometimes lucky to hit the playing card. I checked all of the screws on the rifle and scope mounts; they were all tight. I was told that the barrel was going bad, and as I did not know how much it had been shot before I got it and knowing I had shot it a lot, I began to think the unthinkable. I began to entertain the thought of selling or trading this wonder of wonders to some poor unsuspecting soul before it went completely sour. At this point, I am reminded of the story of the general store keeper in Maine, in the dead of winter and business is very slow. All of the regulars are sitting around the potbelly stove or playing checkers at the back of the store when a man of obvious means walks into the store and states that he would like to purchase a good deer rifle because he, in the haste of packing his gear, left his rifle back home in New York City. The words "New York City" were not lost on all the ears in the back of the store and with that statement it set this poor fellow aside as fair game, "One of those New York sports."

The store keeper took this fellow to the center section of the store, and there on the wall hung a number of shotguns and rifles. All recently cleaned and polished in hopes of a brisk sale due to the opening day of hunting season. The owner reached up and handled the sport a well-used Cal. 30-30 Winchester, Model 94 rifle and told him that he would let him have it for the very low price of forty-five dollars and would throw in ten rounds of ammunition free. The sport was happy with the price and after working the action a time or two said he would take it. Shortly after the sport had left the store, a voice from the potbelly stove area said, "Cyrus, you go to church each Sunday and profess to be a Christian man. So I want to ask you how in heaven's name you could, in good Christian conscience, sell that man a gun for forty-five dollars that has had a twenty-five dollar tag on it for the two years it has been in this store and still call yourself a Christian."

The owner of the store looked at the fellow who had just taken him to task and replied, "Hiram, I am a Christian man and the basis for that last transaction came directly from *The Bible.* You need to read the book of St. Matthew, chapter twenty-five, verse thirty-five. 'I was a stranger and ye took me in.' "

So I, like the store owner from Maine, was only working out my own salvation. The day came, as always, when I found myself standing at the door of Mr. Weinmiller's shop. I stepped inside and after a warm greeting, we began to talk of hunting season excitement and where he intended to hunt. We covered much ground on a wide range of subjects, crops, health, the arms buildup, the cold war, and such, but like courtship the good night kiss is saved till the last moments, so it was with this conversation. I recall that Mr. Weinmiller said, "I see you have your little Hornet with you. Are you going shooting?"

I replied words to the effect, "No, sir, I came to talk to you about perhaps making a swap." At the utterance of this statement, I could see he was taken back a bit, because he knew how much I thought of this rifle. He stated that when I bought it he was sure it had a home for life and thought that for a turkey rifle that I could hardly do better. I have lived long enough at the time I write this to know that when we are less than honest or become outright devious in dealing with friends regardless of the circumstances, we will, somewhere down the path, run into sorrow. Had I been completely honest with him, Mr. J. W. Weinmiller would have solved my problem with this rifle. His experience with shooting problems in all types of firearms was light years ahead of mine. Had I told him of the rapid loss of accuracy in this rifle, he would have asked me to let him have it over the weekend and he would have found that there was nothing wrong with the barrel. But being long in the gun business he knew he could sell this rifle the first week it was in his shop. He asked what I had in mind and I told him that Remington caliber .222 had quite a bit more power and range than the Hornet and that we might work up a trade for the one he had in the gun rack. I also stated that I wanted to keep the scope and mounts. With some consideration, we arrived at a swap.

I put the scope on the Remington .222 and a week and a half later, I had a chance to put it on the sand bags at 100 yards. The rifle was used but appeared to be in mint condition. However, in shooting it, I found that I was getting bullet placement that would not stay on a four-by-four-inch card. I went back to Mr. Weinmiller with my tale of woe and he said he wanted to try the rifle at his range. A week later, after a good workout at his range, he told me that the fault was not with the rifle but with the scope. The scope would not maintain its zero. Once set, it would hold for two or three shots, then would have to be reset. *Oh what a tangled web we weave, when first we practice to deceive.* I asked J. W. if I could buy or trade him again for the Sako Hornet and he told me he had sold it to Dr. Wall, our local dentist.

Dr. Wall was a fine hunter, woodsman, rifleman, and handloader as well as being an excellent dentist and good man. I can't say I was happy but in a way I was glad that he had the Hornet because he would treat it with loving care. I was at a turkey shoot about a month or so after he bought the gun and I asked him if he would entertain the thought of selling the Hornet back to me. He smiled and said that he thought not, then he reached into his billfold and brought out three targets shot with this rifle, at 100 yards. Five shot groups, three-fourths of an inch and some of the holes were touching. I felt a lump in my throat and my eyes began to water. I needed a crying towel and to make it worse I was still the owner of that worthless scope.

The Remington 722A

If your car doesn't run, you take it to a good repair shop. If you have a problem in your plumbing that you can't seem to fix, you call a plumber. Trite, well-worn advice, but think of the time, money, and effort that is lost each day because it is not heeded. It works well on rifles too, and I know a lot of good gunsmiths.

I came by this Remington 722A rifle in a gun trade that I spoke of in another chapter titled "The .22 Hornet." I had read a good bit about the Rememington caliber 222 cartridge and all that I had read about it was very good. It was setting benchrest records in the mid-fifties, one after another, all across the country. The model 722A Rememington rifle that I had swapped the Sako Hornet for was by contrast a very plain Jane rifle. It was tapped for a scope and had low mounted weaver blocks already installed. Unknowingly, I put the defective three-by-five power scope on this rifle and after a short period of grief, I enlisted the aid of someone who knew a lot more than I did at the time of the swap. A new Redfield four power scope with medium cross hairs was all I needed to end my woe. I found this rifle to be extremely accurate, with some five shot groups having all of the bullet holes touching. All of these shots were from a sand bag rest at 100 yards and with three-minute barrel-cooling pauses between shots. In hunting I used fifty-two grain speer hollow point bullets and my turkey load in this rifle was always 2,600 feet-per-second. I used Bal-C powder and standard small rifle primers, CCI or Winchester brands.

I used a reduced load for three reasons. The first one was accuracy. You will get better accuracy with a slightly reduced load, in most instances, than with a max load. The second reason was that a bullet moving a whole lot beyond 2,600-feet-per-second will cause considerable meat destruction. The third reason for loading down is always barrel life. The heat generated by hot loads tends to produce a blowtorch effect. If you have ever watched a person cutting steel with a cutting torch and observed the steel when it reaches a fluid state, you will have seen that at this point the person doing the cutting releases the oxygen to blow the flowing steel away. That is a picture of what happens to a degree in your rifle barrel with loads above 3000 feet per second, especially if the rifle is fired fast, super heating the barrel.

Let's return to the 722A. This rifle was a true tack driver and could be depended on to do its part, every time, at all ranges out to 200 yards. I rarely use any rifle on turkeys beyond this range. However, I shot many crows to 300 yards and, as I have said, it shot like a house on fire. I guess that I would have been more pleased with this rifle had the weight and balance been more to my liking. It did, however, kill turkeys very well when I could hit them, but I did not always do that. I killed a number of turkeys with this rifle and let some get away unwounded, due to my poor shooting but I never lost one I hit. I will say that when one was hit with this load, you could go pick him up because he would be there at the place he was standing when you fired this rifle. Most of the shots I missed with this rifle were due to holding about three inches too high and shooting over the turkey's back. I did this most of the time when I misjudged the distance between my position and that of the bird.

I will relate the results of a hunt that took place north of Oldsmar, Florida, in the spring season of 1966. I was hunting at the invitation of my pal, Les Libby, a water color artist, hunter, woodsman, naturalist, and almost a brother. We were both employed with the Florida Game and Fresh Water Fish Commission at the time this hunt took place. Les, in the performance of his everyday duties, had come across this bit of fine turkey woods north of Oldsmar. The place was ideal. The Florida Power Corporation had a set of power lines that ran north and south for miles and the steel braces that held the lines sat in the middle of a strip that was about eighty yards wide. Standing in the middle of this strip, and looking south, one had the illusion that you could see from that point to the end of the earth.

Live oaks, scrub oaks, cabbage palms, palmetto, and pines comprised the cover and each provided food in season. Small farms and pastures were scattered throughout the area and this along with the power line right-of-way was all that could be asked for in the way of ideal turkey habitat. It was also particularly good as a spring gobbling ground. The small section that we were to hunt on was comprised of about 400 acres and had all of the trees that I have listed and two forty-acre pastures that were not in use at that time. We drove from Tampa the afternoon before the hunt and did a lot of scouting. At the end of the day we sat on the tail gate of the truck and talked a bit. We each had an idea where we wanted to hunt at daylight the next morning. I wanted to hunt to the northwest and Les had found the sign that he wanted southeast of where we were going to start the hunt. We had both seen a lot of turkey signs: dusting mounds, droppings, preened feathers, and plenty of turkey tracks. Many of these tracks were four and a quarter inches long from the front toe to the ball of the heel. It looked so good I had trouble going to sleep that night. In time sleep came and it was very sound and deep when the earth shaking jangle of the alarm clock brought us to life once more.

We put together a stiff brew of coffee, the kind our old time wildlife officers made in an enamel blue and white speckled pot shoved into a bed of hot coals. When it was ready, you could throw a horseshoe in this brew and it would float. Les and I each had a cup of this followed by toast, jelly, eggs, bacon, and one more cup of this eye opener. This second cup would make you snort like a horse. Like the man said, "It's good to the last drop," and after the last drop you were wide awake and ready to go turkey hunting.

We rolled into our spot at just the right the time, and after parking we walked for about fifteen minutes to the point where we parted company. We planned to meet back at this point at 10:30 A.M. to brag, cry, or develop a new battle plan. I had made a blind of sorts the evening before, but the back of it was open and fully exposed from a west view. The side that faced north gave adequate cover as did both the east and south sides. I eased into my blind and, once there, began to wish I had brought more palmetto, broom sage, and Spanish moss to make a better blind.

I shoved five rounds into the rifle and very quietly eased the bolt forward, picking up the last round and easing it into the chamber. I put the safety on the safe position and sat back to await developments. The colors began to change, and the clouds in the east began to turn pinkish. I have always had to fight with myself to keep from calling too early. The awakening of this new day was no exception. I sat in my blind and began to fidget and the longer I sat the more I fidgeted, until the thought *you can't catch a rabbit with your dog tied* passed my mind. So I cut loose the nine-note call of the barred owl. The response was immediate. A turkey gobbled before I quit hooting. I hooted once more and he did it again. I sat still in my blind and let a little daylight ease on into the pasture north of me. This pasture held about fifty acres and there were many scrub oaks and a number of mature pines in the extreme north end of it. It was from this north end that the gobbles had come. I eased into my possible bag and came out with my slate and peg. I rubbed the surface of the slate with the ultra fine sand paper I carry for this purpose, then blew it off, put the cedar peg on the slate at a slight angle, and let it slip under a light pressure. The result with this particular slate and peg is always a perfect cluck, or a purr if I let it drag. If a series of quarter-inch circles are made five or six at a time under proper pressure and speed, a five- or six-note yelp will be produced. If your slate and peg are well matched for tone and your technique good, you should be able to give one or 100 yelps, clucks or purrs—without mistake. It takes time but practice will take you there. The cluck I made was very low, really just to get the feel of the slate. It was getting light now, so I gave two loud clucks followed by four yelps. At this, the gentleman somewhere back in the scrub oaks gobbled so hard he shook the ground I was standing on and he seemed much closer than I had thought or else I was working with two different turkeys. Within the next five minutes, this bird gobbled ten or more times but had not moved a peg. I looked to the east and big daylight was coming fast.

I picked up the slate and clucked twice then followed with a snappy six note yelp. The gobbler came on my last two notes. It was at this point that I saw the turkey running east along the hog wire fence from a large stand of pine trees west of my blind. He had roosted in one of the pines but with my hearing being what it is, I mis-coursed his first gobbling while he was on the limb before flying down.

He ran along the fence in a frantic effort to find a hole or other gap that would bring him to my side of the fence. In a short time this bird was well within rifle range right at 100 yards but to place the cross hairs on his wing butts or pulley bone seemed impossible. He would hardly stand in one place for a second. This bird would stop only long enough to drop his wings, fan his tail, and gobble then would run back and forth along the fence. At last he came to the corner post where the fence turned north and at this point I thought he would fly to the top of the huge red cedar corner post then drop down and head in the direction of my blind. This was wishful thinking on my part, for this fellow, on reaching the corner post, turned and took his back trail running west once more and at this point, I soon lost sight of him. I sat tight and about ten minutes passed. I thought I heard a soft cluck off to my left and after a moment I slowly stood up in my blind to stretch my legs and also to look around. While standing there, I heard another low cluck and this sound caused me to look to the rear of my blind.

Hindsight is always 20-20. I stated at the beginning of this tale that I wished I had added more to the back of my blind when I made it. Now I could not have felt more naked had I been at the governor's ball in jockey shorts. There facing the back of my blind was a gobbler as fine as anyone could ever hope to see. He was about seventy-five yards from me, standing very still and facing me dead on. He sported a beard about eleven inches long and when

I slowly put the cross hairs on his pulley bone, I could also see the long, keen and curved spurs that he carried. I don't believe there was so much as a blade of grass between us. I took a deep breath, let part of it out, and began to squeeze the trigger. At the moment of recoil, I saw this magnificent bird take wing and fly west. I could clearly see that long and heavy beard hanging down in full view, as he departed my area for the safety of the stand of pines that had been his sanctuary the night before and no doubt for many nights in the four or five years he had roamed this area with his brothers and sisters.

I was really let down. I walked over to where he had been standing and could not find one feather or drop of blood. I could not believe that I had missed but it was very obvious that I had. I sat down and hefted my rifle. It felt as heavy as a railroad iron and seemed to have about as much balance.

I put the spent hull into my pocket and began to give some deep thought to the events that had just taken place. In time, I had the foolish notion that I might change my position and go to the edge of the pines in the direction the turkey had flown. Perhaps with a bit of really slick calling, I might entice him out again. It was worth a try. On this thought, I let about forty-five minutes elapse and eased on down the hog wire fence going west.

On reaching the edge of the palmetto flat, I cut enough palmetto fronds to make a snug blind and after putting my hideout together, I relaxed, caught my breath, and clucked on my slate twice, loudly. I heard nothing and after a wait of about ten minutes, I clucked once more and followed it with a six-note yelp. In front of my blind at about forty yards, I thought I saw a palmetto frond sway. I eased my hand over to take my slate off of my knee to make another call and as I did this I knocked it to the ground. I reached down to pick it up and when I raised my head and looked where the frond had swayed a moment before, there was a red head with a white cap sticking above the palmettos.

I could not see this bird's body, only the head and neck. At this point, my heart began to pound hard. I eased the rifle up and said to myself, "If I can get a good picture in the scope, I will try to pull off this neck shot and if I miss, I will miss clean." I let my excitement abate for a second or two as the cross hairs settled on a point halfway down the patch of crimson sticking above the palmettos. I took in a short breath, let a little out, and began to put pressure on the trigger. Once again, the morning stillness was broken by the sharp report of the .222 and once more this wonderful bird took wing flying northwest to a remote part of the pasture where things were much quieter and he could get over the shakes caused by the sweet talk that had almost cost him his life twice in one morning. I guess I should have tried to yelp him up one more time, just to see if I could do it, but at the time I did not feel that I was equal to that task.

I had an uncle by marriage, Sam Poore, who has gone to his reward now, but in his time on earth he killed many, many turkeys. He used a wing bone for most of his life but in his later years he used a very good Gipson-type lynch call with a hinged lid, which I gave him, plus a cedar box call with a cedar striker and chalk that I was making and selling at the time. He was a woodsman with few peers and he knew the Florida wild turkey as well as any man alive as he lived with them on a daily basis. His log cabin home sat in some of the finest turkey woods in the state of Florida at that time. Now this fellow might have yelped up my turkey the third time. I remember that he told me about a turkey he was yelping to with his wing bone. The bird was very cautious and came slowly to a large pine tree that had fallen to the earth in a hurricane a year or two before. Sam had sat on the ground and stuck a few palmetto fronds in front of him and with his back to the fallen tree, continued to cluck and yelp to this turkey.

This bird, as turkeys will on occasion when they come to believe the sounds given by the caller are that of another turkey, threw all caution to the wind and ran up to the back side of this tree. Sam was in a fix or so he said. He had expected this bird to come to the front of the downed pine. He looked downward, observing the space under the tree, and was surprised to see the feet of the turkey standing on the other side of the log. He said that at this moment the thought came to him to reach between the tree and the ground and grab the bird by the legs. His hand eased down and quick as a wink, he had this fellow by the legs. I asked Sam what happened at this point, and he said, "Phil, I began to try to pull this bird under the log and the more I tugged, the more the turkey fought. I came to realize that this was a very big turkey that I had hold of, and I knew that due to his size, I could never pull him under the log."

I asked, "Sam, what did you do to get out of that fix?" "Phil," he said "I did the only thing I could have done. I turned him loose, grabbed my wing bone and yelped him around to my side of the log and shot him." I started using a turkey call when I was in my very early twenties and can do a fair job of calling with almost anything that has been devised thus far to call up turkeys but I feel that I must yield the honors to Sam and his magic wing bone. I will, however, state here that I have called up a number of turkeys and missed them with rifles, and all of them good rifles, and then after a respectable period of time, yelped them back once more. In most cases, I have changed my position fifty yards or so in the direction that the bird ran or flew. I would not have you believe that I have called back every bird that I have ever shot at and missed with a rifle, but I have had a great deal of success in calling back birds I have missed on the first shot.

As a matter of fact, I did this recently. I missed a bird standing at ninety yards across a canal; he flew and then began to run. I put a mouth yelper to the roof of my mouth and began to yelp, cut and cluck. He stopped running and began to gobble. He was a fine nineteen-and-a-half-pound bird but I will speak more of him in another part of this book. I have been most fortunate in my turkey hunting with a shotgun. I have yet to lose a turkey that I have fired at with a shotgun. This is not to say that I have not had to search for twenty minutes or so from time to time in dense foliage in order to find a bird that was not hit well. With the type of shot shells made in the past ten years, lost birds are almost a thing of the past, if one will let the bird come to within forty yards.

The coming of the hardened copper plated shot, polyurethane buffers with plastic wadding, and denser powder that give room for more shot spelled the beginning of a new era in shotgun shooting. In some shotguns, the new premium short magnum shells will pick up the pattern ten to fifteen percent at forty yards. Who knows what can be done with the new twelve gauge three-and-a-half-inch Magnum throwing a full two and a quarter ounces of shot. I have told you of a hunt where I shot at and missed the turkey with the Remington 722A rifle, and now I am going to tell you of a hunt on which I shot and killed a fine young gobbler with this rifle in .222 caliber.

I was hunting once more in a place that always delighted me and was with two people very close to my heart. Lamar Sanders and his father, Cecil, had asked me to make a morning hunt with them in a place called McElvain Hammock. Thirty-five years ago this hammock was at times partially dry but then it could become very wet almost overnight, given two or three inches of rain. I looked at what remained of McElvain Hammock a short time ago and it was bone dry, and well it should be with the drainage program in the county. I had not seen it in twenty years.

Roy Sanders had taken me and my friend Jack Van Dervort on tour of all of the places that I hunted as a young man. We rode through much of the area that I had known like my own back yard but then we came to places that had changed so much I could not recognize them. It was as though I had never been there before! The timber cutting practices have all but destroyed most of the lovely high hammocks that abounded in this area thirty years ago. We stopped at a very large, open flat, got out of the pickup, and stretched our legs. After walking about a bit, I asked where we were and he told me that the flat I was looking at had been one of my favorite turkey haunts, the third Nelson Bay. When he told me this, as I looked out across the treeless, arid wasteland before me, it almost brought tears to my eyes. Tears that one would shed at the last rites for an old and dear friend mingled with the hot tears of rage for the destruction of one of the most beautiful hammocks God ever put on this earth.

Over the years I killed a number of turkeys there including the first mature gobbler I had ever called up and shot. The third Nelson Bay was at that time my concept of the Garden of Eden. Giant live oaks that were half grown when Lincoln gave his Gettysburg Address were numerous and scattered throughout this hammock as were huge sweet gum trees, Florida holly, cabbage palms, and bay trees. The floor of the hammock was covered by ferns and gallberry bushes. The north entrance to the third Nelson Bay was through a bower of gallberry and titi bushes that were so thick you were compelled to bend at the waist in order to get through it. Hip boots were the order of the day in most of the years I hunted there, for it was rarely dry in this section of the St. Regis management area. The water in the trail leading to the hammock was a bit above knee deep at what we called normal conditions.

As I have said before, this country was wet in most years. I recall that the deep ditch on the north side of this hammock was always filled with water, except in 1958 and 1959, both years of extreme drought. It may never be as wet there as it has been in years past, due to many factors that have changed the face of the land. However, I know one thing for sure, the third Nelson Bay will never come back in our life time. It is gone beyond recall. It still takes 200 years to grow a 200-year-old live oak tree. I asked Roy about the condition of McElvain Hammock and was told that it had faired no better. What had once been a game paradise, was now a totally barren strip of ground and before this afternoon was over our guide was to take us on a tour to other places that had enriched my life as a young man beyond any means to express it.

At each place we stopped it was the same: all destroyed. This litany of destruction included Yellow Jacket, Mound Hammock, Coon Ford, Mal Hines Rock Hole, and Garnto Hammock. The last place on the list was the hardest for me to look at. Garnto Hammock had been the place I wanted my ashes scattered and a small bronze plaque with my name, birth and death dates, and a few words I had decided on by De Chardin placed on a huge bay tree that stood at the entrance of the second part of this hourglass shaped hammock. But all of the live oaks, cabbage palms, sweet gums, and bay trees, including the one on which I wanted to place my bronze plaque, were gone—cut down, chopped, and burned. The huge land chopping machine people called "the monster" had been brought in and used to clear the entire area, and then a year or so later they planted young pine trees over all of it. As we drove away from this place that had held so much for me that I treasured, I was almost in a state of shock. I could not bring myself to believe that anyone who had walked through, surveyed or looked at this beautiful bit of land could bring themselves to so completely destroy it.

I asked our guide if we could swing by Pleasant Grove Cemetery and as we rode along I thought of all the turkey hunts I had made in this area when I was a young man. On many of them I returned home without anything but pleasant thoughts and on others I arrived back at my point of departure with a bird in hand, as some of them came very easy. It is about one such easy bird that I now write. I had gone turkey hunting with Lamar Sanders and his father Cecil, and we had ended up at McElvain Hammock by midmorning. We talked for a short bit of time before we agreed to split up and meet just before noon on the trail we had walked in on. I walked to the west for about twenty minutes, clucking and lost calling, ten and fifteen notes at a time, very fast. I sat down in the branches of a dead tree that had fallen and stuck up a number of palmetto fronds I had cut to erect a blind. I yelped, clucked, kee-keed at fifteen- and twenty-minute intervals to no avail. I heard nothing but the calling of crows in the distance and the drumming of the "Lord God," the pileated woodpecker. I sat there until it was almost time to walk back and meet with my companions, then clucked twice rather loudly, and put my slate and peg in my hunting coat pocket. As always, when I am in a fidgeting mood, my mind will race to many things and in this instance I eased the bolt back halfway on the 722 and was pleased to see the reassuring gleam of brass between the bolt face and the chamber. When I looked up, there walking slowly in front of my blind at about sixty paces was a hen and a young gobbler. I eased the bolt home once more and settled the rifle forearm in my left hand and rested the back of my hand across the tree limb in front of me. The four power Redfield seemed to be moving all over that part of Dixie County and the fact that this pair of turkeys were now half hidden by foliage that they were feeding behind did not help the slight case of the shakes that I felt developing. As always we say to ourselves something like this, "When he steps outs from behind that sweet gum tree, I will take him." How often have I told myself this in the past forty years I would not hazard a guess. Half of the time it works, the other half he never steps out from behind the gum tree but walks straight away to another part of the hammock. He may have made you out or perhaps just wanted to go in that direction.

In this case, I feel that this pair of turkeys never knew I was there. They were, however, aware that a turkey had been calling to them just a short time ago and on arriving at this spot and seeing no turkey, they became, as turkeys will, suspicious and walked away. They left my vision as quickly as they entered it. I clucked twice at three-minute intervals and received a cluck and a yelp or two to tell me to come on and catch up with them.

A short time later I eased out of my blind and slipped along the direction the birds had taken. I arrived at the trail a short time later, sat down, and relaxed. In due time, Buster and his father walked up. I stood up and we began to speak of what we had seen in the way of sign and of game. I was relating my tale of woe when a gobbler stepped out on the trail we were all standing on. Buster and his father were facing me and I was facing them, looking over their shoulders at this bird standing ninety yards away. I whispered, "Don't move, but ease down under my rifle, so I can shoot. There is a turkey one-hundred yards down the trail." They looked over their shoulders and on seeing this bird both men kneeled and stuck their fingers in their ears. I eased the rifle up and once the cross hairs settled on the apex of his pulley bone, I squeezed that fine two-and-three-quarter-pound trigger.

As the saying goes, "It was all over but the shouting." We walked down, pacing off yards as we went ninety yards, as it turned out to the point where this fine young gobbler of the year had taken his last walk on this trail through McElvain. An easy bird? Well, yes and no. This was in all probability the same jake that was walking with his sister past my fallen down tree blind. Thus ended a very good hunt with my early teachers and the best of companions. I said that I was more than pleased with this Remington 722A rifle in many respects. The trigger was exceptional, as was the accuracy and the cartridge. The reason that I let this rifle go in a trade was the fact that in my hands it felt unbalanced and overly heavy. My search was still on for a rifle that shot as well and had the light weight and balance of the Sako.

The Wonderful 870

In recent years, now that I am older, I have come to believe that the gods smile on us from time to time, when they know we are really feeling low and need a smile or two. The only twelve-gauge shotgun that I owned had been swapped for a double barrel Ansley Fox in twenty gauge, leaving me without a proper turkey gun. So now I was shopping for a new twelve-gauge and I wanted it chambered for three magnum shells to be used for turkey hunting. I wanted to find a good, high grade double but as always I could not seem to find the gun that fit both my heart's desire and my billfold at the same time.

One day in 1955, I flew into Lakeland, Florida, to attend a game commission meeting that was to be held there the next day. After a short conference with my boss, I was put on call, but was really more or less on my own until the next day when all of the personnel would attend the big meeting. Rudolph (Doc) Dunn, another pilot for the game commission, picked me up and we drove to the town of Lake Wales and had a fine lunch. After lunch, Doc drove me to the shop of a local gunsmith. I do not recall the old fellow's name, but he was a corker. He would become livid with rage when the politics of that era were discussed on both the local and the national level. He was the old time man who had not lost his ability to become outraged at the misuse of public funds and malfeasance in office that we were seeing much of then and that was just the tip of the iceberg. Lord! Would that there were a few more of his kind around today.

We enjoyed some lively conversation and almost had tears in our eyes from laughing so hard at some of his tirades concerning politicians and lobbyists. After a good cup of coffee to get everyone cooled off, our conversation drifted away from our taxes, elections, graft, politicians, and all of the ill effects this had on wages and interest notes and turned to more serious matters. In short, the real problems in life like finding a good twelve-gauge shotgun with three-inch chambers and a full choke tube that would deliver a 75 percent pattern at forty yards with one and seven-eighth ounces of number five or number six copper plated shot. Our volatile host stated that he had such a gun and that it might be for sale. It was his own personal gun. Doc had told me the old man had been a keen hunter up until the past few years but age and the infirmities that sometimes follow it had caught up with him. Now the only trips that he made to his favorite haunts where deer and turkey were plentiful were the trips made when his head was on the pillow in that twilight state that falls somewhere between consciousness and sleep.

He asked if I wanted to buy a gun outright or swap a gun and some cash to boot or do it on a time payment plan with no interest. I told him that the only gun that I had at the time that I might consider swapping was an army surplus M-1 .30 caliber carbine made by Winchester. I told him that I had the rifle only a short time, and really liked it, and would like to keep it because it shot like a house afire; all true statements. When I said the rifle was in mint condition and made by Winchester, I saw his eyes light up like the backboard of a pinball machine. He went into the back room and came back with a Remington 870 Wingmaster pump with ventilted rib full choke and he also had an extra barrel that went with this gun. The extra barrel was plain with no rib. It also had been shortened and had a Weaver choke installed. To fit the weaver choke there were in a case three choke tubes that were bored improved cylinder, modified and full. This barrel was a three-inch magnum also. The long barrel, which was mounted to the gun at this time, was thirty inches long with a ventilated rib, an ivory bead front, and middle sight. It was chambered for a three-inch magnum with a full choke as tight as it was possible to ream one at the time. I wanted a gun that would pattern seventy-five percent and at the time I ran eighty percent patterns with some shells and shot sizes in my hand loads. The gunsmith told me to bring my carbine in the next Monday when I went to our Lakeland office and if it was all that I had described it to be we would trade even.

When I flew home that weekend I could hardly wait to get back to make the swap. I met Doc Dunn at a small grass strip just outside of Lake Wales and once more we went to see the old fellow at the gun shop. He was as eager to see my carbine as I had been to see his 870 Remington. When I unwrapped my little rifle his eyes really sparkled. After he put it to his shoulder and worked the bolt, checking the trigger and looking through the peep sight, I could tell that he was really pleased with this gun. I also knew at this point that the deal was struck already and not a word had been spoken. I told him I had a small surprise for him and then I gave him an additional ten clips to fit his new toy. He said, "Let's shake hands on this if you feel that this is a fair trade." I took his hand and he had a good, firm grip, the kind of handshake that I had expected from him. We all enjoyed a good cup of coffee and some good conversation. He told me that I would be more than pleased with the way this gun shot.

That was as the saying goes, "The understatement of the year." I have shot few guns in my lifetime that have pleased me as much as this one. With the short barrel and using three and a quarter drams of powder and one and one-eighths ounces of shot in a two-and-three-quarter-inch shell and the one-half choke tube in place, it is a very deadly companion in a dove field. I have also found that if doves are flying close, I can remove the choke tubes entirely and shoot straight cylinder bore on twenty-yard birds. Used in this manner, it becomes very wicked, indeed. The modified, full and extra full tubes that came as part of the trade, all patterned well but other than the one-half choke and the modified, I rarely use the others.

This gun was brought home to hunt turkeys and for this use I could have hardly bought a better gun. I put this gun through a lot of cardboard turkey shooting the first weekend after bringing it home, as our gunsmith friend had given me several boxes of three-inch magnum shells in number fives and number sixes and one box of number one buck shots. When I finished testing this 870 Wingmaster, I knew that I had in my hands one of the finest patterning shotguns that I had ever seen. At fifty yards this gun will consistently put fifteen to twenty number five shots in a cardboard turkey, or one with feathers for that matter. I have killed a large number of turkeys over the years with this gun, at ranges from forty to sixty yards, and I have yet to lose a turkey with this gun. I have seen one other shotgun that was choked as tight or that patterned as well and that was a Winchester model 21, owned by Dr. Wall, our dentist in Williston, Florida in 1955. His gun was also a power to be reckoned with at our local turkey shoot. This shoot was held each fall at the Masonic temple in Williston, and always for a worthy cause. I recall one turkey shoot—and I believe the year to be 1956—in which I won seven turkeys on that Saturday. A friend borrowed my gun and shot and he won a turkey on that set. This made eight turkeys won with the 870 that day. Dr. Wall won six birds that day as I recall.

We were shooting at a card four inches wide and six inches long. It cost one dollar to purchase a shell from the range master and this dollar went as a donation. The card was shot at a distance of twenty yards and then the card was collected and put in a box until twenty-five cards had been shot. Each shooter's name had been added before putting it in the box. The winner was the card out of the twenty five that had the most hits on it. A good gun that would really hold the pattern together could do very well.

I think that it was the next fall that they began to shoot at a four-by-six-inch card with a line drawn from top to bottom and side to side forming a cross. The card that had a pellet closest to the center of the cross would win. The winner might have only eight to ten pellets in the whole card but one would be in the center while the other fellow might have forty pellets in the card but be one-eighth of an inch off center. It really made for a better turkey shoot with more fun for everyone but luck played the major part from this time on. However, the tight choke guns still won a lot of turkeys because the odds were with them.

The deer hunting across and west of the Swannee River about the time I became the owner of the 870 was mostly done with deer dogs and shotguns loaded with buckshot. A shotgun that would hold five or six number one buckshot pellets together in any sort of real pattern at forty yards was a thing of pride and joy and one that would hold a pattern of nine or ten shot together at that range might bring about a swap for a team of white mules and deed to the back forty. As with small shots, this ventilated rib barrel threw buckshots in the tightest of tight patterns. I was not a deer hunter at the time I traded for this shotgun but after shooting a few number one buckshot loads at cardboard just to see what it would do, I and all who looked at my cardboard deer targets were impressed. Ninety percent of the shot placement on a deer target at forty yards could be covered by a circle a little larger than a basketball. After looking at all of the cardboard deer, Lamar Sanders said, "Uncle Phil, I know you would not part with a barrel that shoots like this one but perhaps you would leave it to me in your will."

I looked at him and I knew he was serious. I said, "Buster, so be it." However, he did not have to wait until I slipped through this dimension and into my heavenly Garnto Hammock before he received it. I gave him this barrel twenty-five years ago and now his son, Joey, is using this wonderful barrel for much of his hunting. The wheel of life turns slowly but it is sure in its track: first the old gunsmith, then to me, then from me to Lamar Sanders and from him to his son, Joey. Who knows how many will be served well by this one barrel.

We had no spring gobbling season in Florida at the time I traded for the 870 and it was several years before we had our first legal spring hunt. The trade was made in the spring of the year so other than shooting crows over decoys I had no other choice than to wait until the dove season in the fall to give the 870 a proper workout. I found the short barrel with the Weaver choke device to be deadly in the dove field with the short tube marked "1/2 choke" screwed in place.

This gun in the dove field always made me look like a better wing shot than I am. As I said before though, this gun was not brought home to shoot doves and quail, but for the expressed purpose of killing turkeys and at this point I would like to relate the story of the first two turkeys that I shot with this gun.

My wife, Jessie, and I had driven to Old Town, Florida and from there, north to the community of Rock Sink, which lies halfway between Old Town and Branford. We arrived at the home of Cecil Sanders just in time to enjoy a fine meal that his wife, Verdie, set before us. I can't remember all that we ate that evening but I remember venison, chicken, butter beans, field peas, biscuits and cornbread. All of my readers who have spent time around ladies raised in the last generation and on a farm know that they can cook and season food so well that it will make you swallow your tongue. Each platter had so much food on it a trained poodle couldn't jump over it. We men folk all got up at somewhere around four A.M. and the ladies continued to sleep. We had coffee and some of the meat and bread from the feast the night before, a little butter in the plate and homemade ribbon cane syrup poured over this, and two or three biscuits to mop up the syrup and butter after it was well mixed with a fork. Those were the days before any of us ever heard of the word cholesterol or needed to for that matter; good days too, never to be forgotten!

After breakfast, as always, all of the kinfolk asked me to go to the deer woods with them and as always the lure of the big birds came first and I declined the offer. I told them I was on my way to the Third Nelson Bay to check it out. As it worked out I did not reach the Third Nelson Bay that morning. I was driving an old two-wheeled-drive jeep station wagon and in my round I took a little short cut that cost me the morning hunt. I had cut into a dim road behind Mound Hammock and as I rolled along I came to a bad stretch of mud and deep water in the trail. I started to back out of this but began to spin down so I rolled forward then came back fast cutting the rear end to the right and while I got out of my wet spot I high crowned the rear end on a fat lighter stump covered with weeds. I didn't see it and I was really stuck good and proper.

I was glad Miss Jessie had stayed home or I would never have heard the end of this. I looked in the back end for my jack and found that it was gone. I knew that some of the boys would be coming in at lunch time so I walked the quarter of a mile back to the main grade and walked up and down the grade looking for turkey sign and a helping hand that was not too long in coming. A friend stopped with his four-by-four truck and I was loose in a matter of minutes.

After eating my lunch, I drove to a hammock named Yellow Jacket. I spent about two and a half hours there as I had found a lot of fresh sign made by a large flock of turkeys that morning. I could get no reply to any of my calling but I was in hopes that the flock just might come back through and it was also within the realm of reason that another flock could wander in Yellow Jacket that afternoon, for food was there in abundance and many turkeys used this hammock at the time I write of. I finally gave it up and drove as close as I could to the Third Nelson and there I parked the jeep, put on my hip boots and shoved a pair of copper plated three-inch Magnum number fives into the magazine of the 870. Having done this, I dropped a three-inch Magnum load of number sixes into the side port and shucked the round forward into the chamber.

I had to walk a distance of perhaps two city blocks to reach the mouth of the entrance to the Third Nelson. As always the trail ahead of me was as wet as it was dry. I would walk on wet sand for a 100 yards or so and then be in water, six inches to a foot deep for the same distance it seemed. But I ambled along on this path I began to see turkey tracks. The sign had been made by the passage of a sizable flock and I began to perk up as my adrenaline began to flow bringing with it the sharpness of all the senses. I could see water seeping into some of the tracks and as I worked on toward the flock, I could see the water ahead was riled and muddied because the flock had just walked through it. The water on either side of their tracks was as clear as gin and I knew that they had to be just ahead of me.

I will never forget the weather that afternoon. A stiff cold front had gone through the area the night before and while it was chilly and bright and I was enjoying it, I had a lot more wind than I needed for the job at hand. The wind also seemed to be picking up as I eased along and my hat blew off twice. I clamped it down hard on my head so that it almost covered my eyes. I debated about leaving it on the ground till I got back. I didn't want it to blow off while I was trying to kill a turkey. I did not have long to think about my hat, however. Fifty yards from where I stopped to pick up my hat the trail made a slight curve to the right as I was facing west, and this curve ran for perhaps 100 yards. Where the trail straightened out once more was a low dip that was about fifty yards in length or close to this and at that time was filled with water.

When I came to the end of the curve and peeked around I could see about sixteen head of turkeys milling around thirty yards or so beyond the water's edge up on the high ground. I knew at once that they were well beyond the killing range of my shotgun, even though it was a three-inch magnum. I also knew that in a second they were all going to run west down the trail in a flock and to Lord only knew where. I did the only thing I could think of: I shot into the bushes on the left side of the flock and ran in their direction yelling like a banshee. They rose together and flew in all directions.

I followed the flight of one bird with much interest. As he winged his way in the direction of the Third Nelson Bay, I could see very clearly a long and heavy beard hanging down and it was visible until he flew out of sight. I wondered what an old gobbler was doing running with this family flock. I had never seen this take place before at this point in my hunting experience, though I have seen it a number of times since.

I sat down for a while and smoked a pipe full of tobacco. When it was ashes I knocked them out and then eased south down a dim trail that skirted the east side of the Third Nelson Bay. I had only gone a 100 yards or so when I saw a young gobbler of the year, sitting on the limb of a small buck cypress tree. I shall never forget that picture. As the last rays of winter sunset were falling on the turkey and his cypress tree.

I began my sneak to get in shotgun range of the bird. As I stated before, the passage of the cold front had left us with a brisk wind. And the same wind that had removed my hat twice was now making the young gobbler fan his tail like a rudder in order to stay on the limb. He was facing north and the wind was from the north, northwest at about fifteen miles per hour, with gusts to twenty-five. This fellow must have disliked the wind in his face as he changed his position on the limb and faced south. When he did this his tail feathers really flared and he almost lost his balance, going halfway over when the heavy gust hit him. As John Heywood reported in Proverbs, it is "An ill wind that bloweth no man good." The gods had just placed this fellow in my hands for in changing his position and looking south I was able to slip within forty yards of him very quickly. I leaned against a small cypress and waited for the next gust of wind and while he was shifting tail, wings, feet, and at last, head and neck in order to maintain his balance, as harsh as it sounds, I did what I gone there to do. My eye looked along the back of the receiver, lining the mid ivory bead sight with the front one and I touched off a load of copper plated three-inch magnum sixes, compliments of Olin and company. He never knew what hit him. I sat at the base of the cypress he fell from and had a pipe full of tobacco once more. He was a fine, acorn fat bird of the year, about fourteen pounds. As the sun sank lower, the wind diminished somewhat, except for gusts and I could hear a turkey yelp now and then. I took out a small box call that had been made for and given to me by Richard Wallace, one of the best turkey hunters who ever made track in the sands of the state of Florida. It was an exceptional call that sounded just right to a turkey. I hit a loud cluck followed by about six loud and snappy yelps. I had answers from four different turkeys, and they all seemed to be scattered along the east side of the hammock just inside the Third Nelson Bay. I waited ten minutes then yelped once more. I knew that I was not likely to see another bird that evening and the calls I gave were not given with this in mind. I only wanted to locate as many turkeys as I could in order to know where to make my morning hunt.

I went to sleep that night feeling good about the coming day. After coffee and a good breakfast, we all wished each other luck and I headed to the Third Nelson. It was still dark as I bent over and made my way south through the gallberry and titi tunnel that led into the magnificent hammock that was part of the Third Nelson Bay. After wading knee deep water and being in a half crouched position for half the length of a football field, it was good to step into the hammock and stand up straight. Once inside the hammock, everything was dry. The floor of this bit of woods had a lot of ferns growing there, plus water oaks, black gum trees, sweet gum trees, cabbage palms in all stages of growth, and many 100- and 200-year-old live oaks. All in all, it was a place that you enjoyed being in, whether you saw a turkey or not, because the scenery was incomparable. I eased around in the half light, cutting a few palmettos to build my blind and in doing so caused a turkey to leave the roost and fly to the outside of the bay in the direction I had killed the young gobbler the evening before. While I did not have all of the palmettos I wanted for my blind, after the turkey flew, I knew I had all I was going to get at that time. I stuck the ones I had in a semicircle in front of a huge sweet gum tree, cut ten or fifteen ferns and placed them, making sure that the barrel on my shotgun had a two-foot clearance all the way around once I was seated inside my blind. I set out the cedar box call on some dry Spanish moss, along with my chalk and striker. I put the six-twelve bottle close at hand as I knew the insects would be bad at sunrise. I slipped an army head net over my hat, sat back, and awaited developments. They were not long in coming.

Turkeys began to fly from everywhere within the hammock. The strange thing about this was that instead of flying down and feeding in the hammock as I had expected they would, they were each flying to the outside of the hammock and meeting on the road. This was easy to read from the sign that I saw when I came out of the bay later that morning. I sat there wondering what to do, and it began to look like what I thought would be a sure thing and an easy hunt was about to turn into a hard one. I chalked the lip on my box call and also the striker. I put the little box that Richard Wallace had made for me in the palm of my hand and cut loose a pair of good clucks. I received an answer within a heartbeat. The bird that came to my clucks did so with clucks of its own. And so it was back and forth, I would cluck, then the turkey would cluck. This exchange continued for the better part of twenty minutes in three-minute intervals. Then this bird began to leave me. It would go southwest of my blind and almost out of my hearing, clucking as it went.

I kept up my part of this clucking contest and the turkey would turn and come back only to leave and repeat the pattern. After this had occurred about three times, I heard this turkey really covering ground coming back. It would cluck and then the next time it clucked it seemed to be thirty yards closer. I got my gun across my knee and pushed off the safety. I gave one more call, a cluck, and then I saw a red head sticking up out of the ferns.

Once again as I had done the evening before I looked down the rib and placed the ivory beads on this bird's head and neck then touched off the charge. There was a great flailing of wings and flouncing about on the hammock floor. I thought, *This fellow sure is raising cane for a young turkey.* Then I got up and paced off the distance from my blind to the bird. It was thirty-five yards. I reached down into the ferns, and they were quite thick there, and took hold of my bird, the one I had believed to be a jake all of the time I was working him. He was the bonus bird, the fellow that I had seen flying with his beard hanging down! This was my first big gobbler. He weighed nineteen and a half pounds, had an eleven-inch beard that had very full, sharp, and curved spurs that were one and a half inches long.

I took his beard and spurs to Steve Fickett, a friend of mine who was a Florida Game and Fish biologist, and he was of the opinion that this bird was five years old. I recall a hunt made in the early 1960s when I again was hunting in a place that bordered the St. Johns River on the west side below the community of Deer Park, Florida. I had obtained permission from a ranch owner to camp and hunt turkeys on his property. This hunt had been planned a week ahead, so on Friday evening after work I set up camp and got all of my gear ready for the next day. I awoke the next morning to a howling gale. The trees and bushes around my camp were all leaning backwards. Winds blew twenty miles per hour with gusts to thirty-five. Although there was no rain in sight, I did not hold much hope for a very successful turkey hunt on this day. After a good, hot cup of coffee and a breakfast of bacon and eggs with toast made in my reflector oven, I began to feel a little better about the weather conditions and began to believe that I might just be able to walk up on a flock of turkeys in one of the small cabbage palm hammocks that were everywhere throughout the area. I pulled on my hip boots, knowing that I had one canal to cross and then Lord only knew what else, because water had been high that fall. I picked up the 870, my stool with the bag below it that contained all of my calls and light gear, and headed west across the marsh. I crossed the canal that had worried me but found that I had no need for mental reservation because the water was not as deep as I had thought. I crossed without spilling a drop of water over my boot tops.

In a walk of about thirty minutes I reached the first hammock in my line of travel. I slipped into it and was sure that with the wind condition being as it was that it would be just as difficult for a flock of turkeys to hear me as it would be for me to hear them. With this thought in mind, I left my caller in the bag attached to the bottom of my stool. I felt that on this day it would all have to be done by eyesight and there the turkeys had the edge. A turkey, I have read and I myself am sure, sees movement much better than we do and a flock of ten turkeys sees ten times better. But there are two other major factors to be reckoned with: blind luck and the element of surprise. I crept through this hammock then through five or six others as the early part of the morning slipped away. The turkeys were nowhere to be found and on the ground that I had covered, sign was almost nonexistent. I was beginning to get a bit discouraged.

As I worked farther west the land became more elevated and was somewhat drier. At this point I began to pick up a little bit of sign, here and there. The farther west I traveled the better the signs became and although the wind had blown the sand this way and that, I could still make out what I believed to be the passage of eight head of turkeys, walking in a westerly direction ahead of me. If I was correct in my assessment, this flock had roosted in one of the hammocks I had walked through earlier and was now marching in the same direction that I was headed. If they continued this march it would lead them to an old cow pen on the property, no longer in use.

A quarter of a mile from where I found this first bit of sign was a narrow trail that ran between two huge railroad ties that had formed one of the entrances into the old cow pens. As I stood looking downward in the sand between the cross ties I saw sure sign, just made by this flock. I stepped through the gap and when I did so I saw six turkeys standing thirty yards northwest of my position. I quickly put the ivory beads on a fine young gobbler and when they lined up and became one, I squeezed the trigger.

The five other turkeys flew to the west, and as I looked at my gobbler, I could see that he was not alone in his last dance. Behind a screening of palmettos, a mature hen and another gobbler of the year were making their last futile efforts to depart the cow pen. I had not the foggiest notion that the two birds were behind the palmettos when I shot. They were quite close together at the time of the shot and had they not been, the pattern at thirty yards out of this set of barrels was so tight I am sure that I would have missed them.

I know a man who was fifteen years of age when he killed five very old, long-bearded gobblers that were feeding in a dried up cypress pond, somewhere across the Swannee River. He was using a Sears Roebuck, J. C. Higgens, twelve-gauge pump gun, which he had worked very hard to buy. He had spotted them feeding, and taking his time, he crawled up to where he could get three of them with their heads together. He shot them then pumped in a new round for each of the other two gobblers. He got them all. This was youth. I am sure that today this fellow would never do this even if it were possible.

He was in his twenties when he told me this story and his reputation as a hunter in the area at that time was already a legend. He advised me never to do as he had done, if I ever had the opportunity. They were an additional ninety pounds along with your gun and any other gear you had to carry. He had to go get an uncle to bring a tractor to take him and his once-in-a-lifetime bag of turkeys home. One of the turkeys his uncle received as payment for services rendered. My killing of the two extra birds was purely accidental but it did not make the three of them weigh any less. I had three miles of marsh to traverse and no uncle with a tractor to help me with this chore, so I ended this hunt along the St. Johns River. It was a fine one.

The next hunt took place northwest of Old Town, Florida, in a very favored place called "Coon Ford." What a shame that we have to live half a lifetime before we can really begin to see and hear. It was a brilliantly bright day, the kind where all of the colors seem intensified and even the sounds of birds in the hammock seemed amplified in volume.

Along about nine-thirty I heard a sound that needed no amplification for my ears. I had heard what sounded like a small dog barking about 200 yards back in the direction of Mound Hammock. This barking was answered by two or three other small dogs. The one dog kept it up for a minute or two, then all was quiet for five minutes. The next time I heard the dog, his barking had turned into the yelping of a turkey and from the time I last heard it yelp. I do not believe two minutes had elapsed before the trail behind me and to my right was filled with turkeys. They had run onto this flat in a rush and were now milling around everywhere about me.

I had two hens that were really giving the back side of my blind the once over. The gallberry bushes to my back were thick, but there were some small openings. As hens will, this pair began to crane their necks and one even put her head almost inside my blind. I had on a face mask and my hat was pulled down low over my eyes so I sat tight. With some cutting and pit pitting to show her displeasure, this hen and her sister ran out on the flat to feed before coming back to loaf in the shade, then to dust and loaf again before feeding once more, on their way to the roost. I could not see one turkey from my position. They were all to my left side feeding on a palmetto flat that was shielded from my view by high gallberry and titi bushes.

I said to myself, "I am going to put this flock in the air and scatter them proper," and in saying this I fired my gun into the ground in front of me and turkeys went to all points of the compass. I had two more three-inch shells in the magazine, and I will never know why I held them both back, but I reached in my hunting coat and picked up another shell marked #5-3. I dropped it in the ejection port and shoving the other rounds back beyond the holding peg, I shucked the new round into the chamber. I stepped out on the flat and saw a turkey sitting in a pine tree at the other side of the flat east of my blind. As a general rule I am good at estimating range for both shotgun and rifle but, as I stated in the beginning of this tale, it was one of those very bright days where colors seemed to jump out at you and all things seem closer than they are.

I looked at the turkey in the tree once more and putting the ivory bead on its head, I blew my flute, lifted the lid, and let the cobra out of the basket. At the sound of the shot the turkey tumbled end over end. It was killed so dead that it did not even quiver. It seemed strange to me that there would be no more reaction than this from a bird shot at what I believed to be at least sixty yards at the time. As always, I was pacing the steps as I walked to this bird and I found to my surprise that from the edge of my blind where I had ejected the shell that had killed this bird it was not sixty yards but seventy-two. When I got back to the blind I picked up the shell that had killed her, for it was a hen that I had shot, which was legal to shoot at the time. In looking at this spent shell I saw that it was one I had hand loaded with deer as well as turkeys in mind. I had opened up the crimp, poured out the lead shot, and replaced it with some number five copper-plated shot and three number one buck shot pellets then buffered all of this with old fashioned corn meal.

I drove back to Cecil's house for lunch and when I dressed this bird, I found that she had been hit by all three number one buck pellets, in a five-inch pattern. No wonder she never quivered. At seventy-two yards, hit by all three pellets, do you think the gods were smiling on me that morning or was it all luck—perhaps both! A good tight choke, a lot of luck, and the smile of the gods! I am sure all three elements were in effect that day with luck perhaps playing the largest part.

The hunts I have related to you thus far in which I have used the Remington 870 have all been hunts made in the fifties, sixtees, and very early seventies. I will tell you now of two hunts that took place more recently using my old sweetheart and a new set of barrels.

About ten years after my gun trade in Lake Wales, I began to get the "what if" feeling. I am sure all who read this have had a touch of this virus at one time or another in their lives. The day comes when you say to yourself "What if the barrel on this gun was only twenty-five or twenty-six inches long, but still was choked as tight and had a ventilated rib." I saw this gun in my mind's eye and it looked just right to use inside a turkey blind. I sat down and wrote a letter to the customer gun work department of Remington Arms. I told them of the unbelievable choke in the long barrels of the 870 that I owned and of the patterns that it shot out to sixty yards, stating that I would like very much to have them duplicate this set of barrels in every respect but in a shorter version perhaps as short as twenty-five inches and if not that, twenty-six inches. In due time I received a very polite letter stating that as much as they would like to help me out with this, they could not. Well, I had killed quite a few turkeys, ducks and Lord only knows how many squirrels with this set of barrels at this time so although I wanted a short tight-choked barrel for this gun, I felt in no way handicapped.

I will say, at this point, that it took the boys at Remington Arms about another twelve years to realize that I was not the only one out there who wanted a set of short barrels for his 870. I think that it was about 1977 that Remington Arms proclaimed to one and all that they were offering a tight, full-choked, short barrel for the 870 Wingmaster that was designed for turkey hunting.

I placed my order soon after reading the advertisement and in about two weeks my package arrived. I knew that there was no ventilated rib with this barrel but I never expected it to look so plain. It was short, only twenty-six inches and chambered for two-and-three-quarter-inch shells instead of three-inch. I had hoped for three-inch Magnum but I had been using two-and-three-quarter-inch short Magnum shells with one and a half ounces of shot in other shotguns, and after reading that there was only a twenty pellet difference between the one-and-a-half-ounce short Magnums and the three-inch one-and-five-eighths-ounce shell, I was not too upset.

Let me say now that once I took this barrel to the field for a session on the patterning board and after having examined the turkey patterns shot with it from ten yards on out to sixty, using four, five, and six shot sizes, I was more than pleased. After counting the number of hits made with fives and sixes in short one and a half magnum loads at the fifty and sixty yard range as well as the head and neck shot count, I began to feel that it was close to being as good as the old set of barrels at the shorter ranges.

Up until the 1990 season I believed it to be all the turkey gun that a fellow needed in a single-barrel, pump-action shotgun. Then a friend of mine, David Streicher, came by my house about the second week into the spring gobbling season. On this occasion he brought with him a new Mossburg 835 pump, twelve-gauge with three-and-a-half-inch chambers in a twenty-inch barrel, with vent rib and full factory camo finish, with all metal parts sand-blasted and nonreflective. The three-and-a-half-inch shells looked like Roman candles. This gun throws a pattern of number four shots at sixty yards that has to be seen to be believed. No turkey is going to live through it once this lightning bolt is turned loose on it at any reasonable yardage. I wish David had left this damn gun at his house when he made that visit. It is about to cause me to spend some money that I had put aside for my grandson's education, among other things.

Well, enough of the Star Wars pyrotechnics. Let us return to the spring gobbler hunt on Turkey Island as a guest of Mr. Charles Strange. I had called my constant hunting companion Jack Van Devort the evening before, but he had a previous engagement that left him no way out, so on this hunt I would be alone. I am really not adverse to hunting by myself. I took my gear and my gun and headed for my favorite spot. I walked down the sand road east of the hog pen a 100 yards then followed the road as it turned and went south, another 125 yards. This brought me to the place I liked best on the island.

This place had a small round field about sixty yards in diameter, bordered by cypress swamp almost completely around it except for the northernmost tip of the field. A twenty-foot-wide band of palmettos, blackjack oaks, cabbage palms, and live oaks lined this tip running east to west, and paths through this band of trees lead into the other sixty yards round field that lays to the north. Gobblers and hens use both fields as a trysting ground. In gobbling season you will see many fresh dust mounds, tracks, feathers and drag marks where gobblers have let their wing tips drag in short circles while strutting in the sand.

On this morning after looking at the last round field I decided to hunt the first field because I liked the amount of sign that I was looking at there. I went to the extreme west side of the round after placing my flambeau hen decoy alongside a cabbage palm that had fallen on the ground but was still alive with the tree portion turned up at the end and growing much the same as any other cabbage palm. After setting "Peggy Sue" in a position I thought would look good to a lovestruck gobbler, I eased on back twenty-six yards and then erected my blind ten yards or so back in the ti-ti bushes in deep shade. After draping it with bits of Spanish moss and some broom sage, and sticking a few palmettos in front, my camo-blind looked good. I crawled inside, put my back to a cypress tree, and hooted like an owl.

No turkey gobbled but several owls began laughing all at once all around my blind. A little later I sort of catnapped a bit and when I woke up I looked at my watch and fifteen minutes had slipped past. It was almost 6:30. I pulled my wing bone out and cut back on it. I clucked four or five times then yelped six or eight times. I had a gobble for an answer and then another. I cut four or five times, and he would gobble and I could tell that he was on the way. I yelped with the wing bone trumpet once more. After the next gobble I put the bone away and took out my slate and peg. The next time this bird gobbled, he was only fifty yards away. I clucked low twice, purred, and followed it with three yelps that were hardly audible to human ears. I put my slate and peg on the ground beside my stool and put the 870 across my lap. It seems that as soon as I picked up my gun, he chose that time to burst out of the cypress swamp and onto the flat where I was seated, making very large strides in the direction of the hen decoy. On reaching what was to be his destination, he ran right up to the decoy and as he stood there eyeing his new found love. I eased the short barrel through the shooting port in the netting, and the short Magnum load of 4 × 6s traveled the thirty-six yards to this lovesick old boy before he could blink an eye. I walked over to where he lay, I looked at my watch and it was 6:50 A.M.

So this bird fulfilled his destiny, as many before him have, in high style, and in doing so made a lot of people happy, as well as the fellow that shot him.

I could tell many other stories of turkeys called up and shot with this Remington pump with the old set of barrels before they were given to Lamar Sanders, but as with the last story we will not dwell on the past but will return now to Turkey Island and a hunt that took place in the gobbling season of 1989. One of the real pleasures that comes as a bonus when hunting as a guest of Charlie Strange is the roundtable discussion that always takes place after each hunt. I might add that it can take place the morning or afternoon before the hunt also. Some of the conversations are dandy. This is especially so when Mr. John Quincy Adams takes exception to some of the governmental regulations we are treated to from time to time, as handed down by one agency or another. When Quincy's face gets red and he starts to point his finger as he warms up to the subject at hand, and you may believe that the conversation is about to liven up. But we all take our turns. These informal get-togethers take place at the home of Lyle Griffin who provides coffee and cakes, and feeds fire into the conversation or debate when it starts to lag. Fred Cox can be relied on to help Lyle in giving Quincy the needle from time to time. Fred has a nice over and under twelve-gauge and he breaks us all up with the story of buying this gun cheap because it was made wrong. They had one barrel up on top of the other and he had a hell of a time learning to shoot it by turning it sideways.

Charlie Strange and Fred almost always arrive together and Jack Van Devort and I make up the other team. We have a lot of fun and good times. In winter a huge fire is always burning in Lyle's front yard with a very large iron pot full of peanuts hanging over it. A coffee pot is shoved into the coals to one side. With all of the members of this little club sitting around the fire, laughing, talking, drinking coffee, eating boiled peanuts, and the endless teasing of first one then another that goes on, it makes for a warm feeling not brought on by the fire. When we all get together, God is in his heaven and all is right with the world.

But now let me tell you of the hunt on Turkey Island. My hunting buddy, Jack Van Dervort, has killed a lot of turkeys in his home state of New York and also in the area of Pennsylvania where his hunting camp is situated. The method used in his area is that of posting two or three men on one side of a corn field behind a stone fence where turkeys are feeding and having one or more men walk slowly to the turkeys from the opposite side of the field. The drivers take a shot if they can get one in range but it is the men who are positioned as standers that get a shot as a general rule. The men who hunted turkeys in that area also made corn shock blinds near a gap in one of the old stone walls over 100 years ago and turkeys were walking through them each day. As they come by the boys take one or two from the flock. No one from the area ever owned a turkey call or knew how to use one. When Jack told me this, I took it as my Holy Grail to further his education along these lines. The story that follows is about his first day in the one room school house with camouflage netting walls, and when we picked up a piece of chalk it was to be used on a very small slate blackboard, three inches by four and a half. A lot of problems had been worked out and solved on this little blackboard over the years and I was hoping we would solve one on this fine spring morning too.

We were on Turkey Island in a spot we refer to as the last sand round. We call it that because it is literally the last southernmost round open spot at the end of the sand road we walk in on.

In gobbling season, if not disturbed, you can bet that a gobbler and his entourage of hens will be there some time each morning or afternoon. I had talked with Mr. Quincy Adams in regards to the area he intended to hunt on this morning and informed him that if he was not intending to hunt on the last round then we intended to do so. Quincy assured me that this was ok with him, as he wanted to hunt south along the property line.

All of this conversation had taken place the night before the school bell rang and classes started. Jack and I unrolled my blind, stuck the steel rods into the sand, cut a few dog fennel and palmetto fronds, and added a little Spanish moss, and all in all it looked good. We walked over to about twenty-five steps southeast of our blind and set out "Peggy Sue," the hen decoy. Her placement was always dictated by the fact that an approaching gobbler could see her but that no other hunter could come and shoot the decoy from an angle that would put part of the shot charge into our blind. I want to stress now the importance of looking at your blind site the evening before with an eye to safe calling and hunting. If you use a decoy, always sit it in a place where no one can creep up on and shoot in the direction of your blind. God gave you two eyes so use them. Don't position yourself where a load of number sixes might take one or both of them or your life. Be careful!

Once Jack and I were in the blind, we sat back and took a cup of coffee from his thermos and after a sip or two, I hooted the eight-note call of the barrel owl, and while we did not hear a gobble, an owl flew in and sat almost directly over our heads. We played with him for ten minutes or so til we had him and Lord only knows how many others laughing all around us. We sat there enjoying all of this until that time came when a hush fell over the swamp, as it always does just before the crow, the red bird, the thrasher, and in fact all things living there begin to wake up and start a new day. It's a wonderful time to be in the woods even for one that detests getting out of bed early. Along about this time I thought I heard a vehicle stop by the hog pen where we parked our cars to walk back in and a short time after, Jack asked me if I could hear a turkey yelping.

Flying on a daily basis for the Florida Game and Fresh Water Fish Commission in planes that were hardly better sound insulated than an open cockpit, plus firing tens of thousands of rounds of .30- and .50-caliber machine gun bullets, .20-cal carbine, .45 auto pistols, and

30-06 rifles in a lifetime of shooting, and we haven't touched on skeet ranges, dove fields, quail hunting, duck and goose hunting had all taken their toll. In short, when Jack asked if I could hear a turkey I said no. Then he asked if I heard the turkey gobble and my reply was once more in the negative. When he whispered to me the next time he said that he thought it might be Quincy that was yelping and that the gobbler had answered him twice. I thought that at this stage I had better throw my hound into the race so I pulled out my wing bone trumpet call cut loose two loud clucks and about six loud snappy yelps.

Jack said, "Did you hear the gobbler answer you?" I replied in the negative. Then I licked my lips placed the bone just right and tested it as I always do with a low cluck. If this cluck comes out good then I let it rip and never worry about giving a false call. I cut about four times and yelped five.

Jack touched my knee and whispered, "The turkey has quit gobbling to the yelping Quincy is doing with his slate but every time you yelp and cluck on the wing bone he tears up the earth." But I still could not hear his last gobble.

I rested the call for five minutes then clucked moderately loud and gave three half volume yelps. And I heard the gobble! It was only about 100 yards away. I let the wing bone hang from its lanyard and picked up my slate and peg. I looked over at Jack. He was excited and smiling from ear to ear. I was sort of happy myself but I had done enough of this in my lifetime to know that we were not home free yet. A lot can happen in that last 100 yards.

I began to purr and give low pit-pit calls along with the purring. He gobbled once more and Jack touched my knee once more. I saw the quick movement of a red, white, and blue head northeast of our blind about seventy steps away. He was circling our position and when he reached a point thirty-five yards south of the route he was taking he would see "Peggy Sue." It took only one more series of purrs and low yelps and there he stood in front of our blind.

I know we all do foolish things from time to time and we know that it is foolishness when we do it but excitement, carelessness, and Lord knows what else sometimes possess us. I reached down and instead of placing my thumb on one side and my forefinger on the other side of the crossbolt safety as I pushed it into firing position (when done in this manner it makes no sound), I merely shoved the crossbolt safety hard to the left with my forefinger. In the silence of the early morning quietness, this sounded like a gandy dancer hitting a railroad spike with a nine-pound hammer. At this our fine feathered friend stood bolt upright for about one second then turned and ran east as fast as he could go on the exact path that he came in on. I leaned out of the right hand side of our blind as fast as I could and gave this fine old boy the contents of the 870's chamber, a load of Remington short Mag. 4 × 6s. The load reached him at thirty-seven steps and he was dead within the batting of an eye. We walked over and picked him up.

Jack said that this was one of the most exciting days of his life. Being the woodsman and hunter that he is I knew he was hooked already. We were more than pleased with the events as they had taken place, and it was, indeed, Mr. John Quincy who had stopped by the hog pen and could not resist making a call or two but he had given it up when the bird started coming our way.

The bird was a good one. He weighed nineteen pounds and had a nine-inch beard and inch-long spurs. He was hit with forty-seven pellets. As I recall eight were in the head and neck. We loaded our gear, admired the gobbler once more, and headed for Lyle's front porch to sit and sip coffee, and to tell and retell each part of the hunt as I am sure hunters have done since man first learned to communicate.

As you may have surmised by now, I have a very special place in my heart for this old gun that will—lacking three more years—have been one of my main hunting companions for forty years. Other than replacing the recoil pad, it has never given me one bad moment in the field. I would guess that unless I buy one of the new side-by-side double barrels that are being made in three and a half inch Magnum or if I do not use the Ansley Fox this gobbling season, the Remington 870 and I will be doing business on the same old stand.

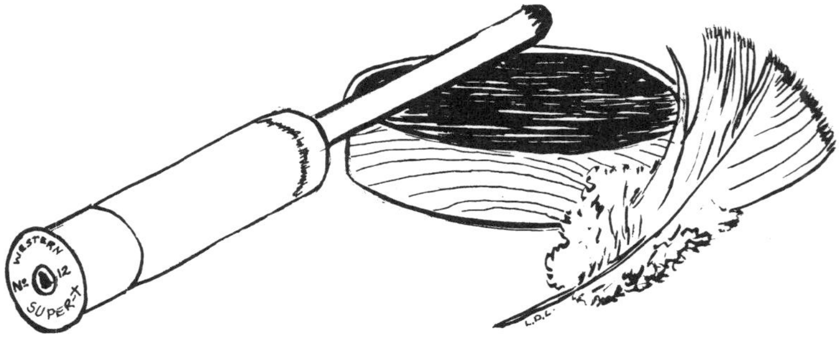

Western #12 Super-X shotgun shell

A Martini Doesn't Always Have to Be a Drink

One day in the mid-sixties, I drove to Ocala, Florida to visit with a friend of mine, a master gunsmith. His name was John W. Knope. We spent a long afternoon and as always covered a lot of ground in a very pleasant conversation ending with my request that he give some thought to building me a first rate, single-shot turkey rifle that would weigh no more than six and a half pounds, when scope mounted. This hickory nut had been rolling around in the back of my head for a long time. Before I departed his shop, he had shown me a B.S.A. 310 cadet single-shot rifle on a small Martini action and a blank .22-caliber Douglas Premium barrel that would have to be machined to fit this action and chambered for a suitable cartridge. We ended up choosing the 218 Mashburn Bee as John had the chambering reamers on hand. The Mashburn Bee was chosen not so much for the cartridge itself, but due to the fact that both the 218 Bee and 25/20 brass was readily available and inexpensive. The case was easy to fire form and with fifteen grains of the old bal-c powder and a fifty-two-grain speer hollow point bullet plus a cc1 small rifle primer you were into the turkey rifle business in good fashion. With the above loading, the bullet leaves the barrel at 2,400 feet per second, or thereabouts. I have found the loading given above to be a good turkey killer, but not too destructive. That's something to think of when the end product is to be placed on a platter in the center of the table.

I will say right off that I would have preferred a .22 K hornet barrel, but hornet brass was not always easy to come by and we had no reamers so we settled on the bee. The two cases were easy to fire form and the case life is a joy, lasting as long as fifteen to twenty firings with the loads I settled on. I will say that I believe the long case life I have always had with brass used in the rifle is due to the relatively low loading of the powder used, which is the first batch of bal-c that was marketed. I feel that another plus given by the loading I use is the fine bullet placement I have always been able to bring off from the bench and in the field. As I write this, I think of many groups that I have shot at targets from 100 yards and also at turkey targets at 125 yards, and the thoughts are pleasant ones. This rifle may not always shoot minute of an angle at 100 yards, but it has done it on many occasions and it can always be depended on to put five shots into one-and-a-quarter-inch groups on the wing butt section of a cardboard turkey silhouette, and the same thing could be said of the bird that wears feathers. As I said before I wanted a 22 K hornet, but I have come to love this little rifle like a brother and with it I have killed a wagon load of both turkeys and wild hogs. This rifle has seen much use and travel in its time. It was made in Birmingham, England, at the Birmingham Small Arms Factory.

When the day came that John Knope put this rifle into my hands, I was elated. I had told him that I wanted a no frills, short, lightweight turkey rifle; one that I could snap a carrying strap onto and take to the woods on my shoulder as I carried my shotgun in my hand, and he had made just that. The gun is not the best looking one of its kind that I have ever seen. I have seen a few rifles of this type made up with fiddle back maple stocks and forearms and even some with good, flame grain walnut stocks and fore ends, but we had decided to leave the British military stock and forearm on the barrel and action because this gun was sure to see hard use. We tapped the barrel and placed Waver blocks and rings on a four-power Redfield scope with medium cross hairs. This rifle pleased me in every way. It was the perfect tool for what it was intended for. I have owned this little rifle since the mid-sixties and my feelings have not changed. I might, perhaps, if it were possible, change it from a single-shot to a three-shot capability and yet I am not really sure of that either. I have had to shoot a second time at both wild hogs and turkeys more often than I would care to admit, but always due to my excitement, not due to the rifle, and I never felt pressed for time. In hunting I have the gun loaded and I keep three rounds under a wide rubber band at the base of the chamber. For a fast second shot, I eject the fired round and the falling block of this rifle is then wide open. I pull the next live round from beneath the rubber band, drop it into the open breach and the shell sails down a groove in the breach block and into the chamber. I lift the lever and it is cocked and ready to fire. All this is done much faster than it takes to write this sentence.

I recall a hunt that I participated in after I had owned this rifle for about two years. I had obtained permission to kill several wild hogs on a piece of property along the St. John's River marsh, west of the town of Sebastian, Florida, and as a matter of fact the ranch foreman would have been pleased if we had been able to kill every hog on this property. The owner had developed a large portion of this land and for five years it had been set out in citrus grove. He also was developing another large tract that was to be put into citrus, and it was on this tract that the hogs were destroying the new grove development by rooting it up almost as fast as it could be cultivated. In short, he was delighted to let two or three of us hunt there at any time it was convenient for us to come. Since this is a book about turkey hunting, I will not belabor you with all of the details of this hunt, but my old compadre Les Libby took the north side of the pasture and I took the southwest. It was my good fortune to trail up the drove of hogs we had set out to find and when I glassed them, I found six hogs that were in the 200-pound class feeding on an open flat seventy yards west of the canal bank that I was standing on. After the smoke cleared and it was all over, I felt somewhat like the old time buffalo hunters must have felt. I had fired my Martini six times at four hogs and they all lay on the ground in front of me. The action had been faster than fast. I had not fired at the other two hogs as I knew we would have a devil time getting the four I had killed back to camp. We ended up getting a grove tractor to get them to camp. I had shot two of the hogs twice as there was a great deal of spinning around, short sprints, and flat out running after the shooting started, all of this making my first shots somewhat ineffective on these two animals. This action took place in a matter of seconds once it got started. I write of this hunt only so that my reader may come to feel as I do that I was under no handicap whatsoever with this little single shot.

It is through many hunts over a long span of time that we come to love a certain shotgun or rifle and will choose it over any of the other guns we may own when we head for the woods. Each of us differ in our reasoning about many things in life, but most of the seasoned hunters I have known and from all walks of life have one or two guns that no amount of money can buy, even if they may be the doggiest guns they own. Some may have a wall in their den that is lined with guns, some with wood so fine and metal so beautifully engraved that they would make your eyes bug out and yet many of these guns are traded or sold off from time to time. But if you look close, you will find two or three in the rack that show quite a bit of wear, not abuse, but honest wear and these are the man's true loves, the ones he hunts with and has for years. They are the ones he depends on. The Knope 218 Mashburn Bee has reached this status in my gun rack and not without reason.

I recall very well the first turkey that I killed with this rifle. I had seen him strutting in a pasture next to a lake that I was spraying with herbicide from an airplane. With each load I carried from the air strip, I crossed this bird's gobbling ground in my path of flight. The more I watched him, the more I wanted to watch him but my thoughts now were that of watching him through a four-power Redfield scope. When my morning's work was finished, I taxied the aircraft over to the main office, and after a short conversation with the property manager, I obtained permission to hunt this gobbler.

I flew home that weekend and after a long talk with my wife, one in which I had to promise to do everything that she felt needed doing for the next six months and some that didn't, I was told that she would not feel too hurt if I stayed out overnight on the coming Friday in order to yelp up this fine bird Saturday morning. Monday morning as I left the house to go to the airport, I reached a pitch of excitement where I almost felt I didn't need an airplane to fly. The week went well and the weather remained perfect. We were able to spray two lakes and one river that week, and from the air I watched this fellow gobble and strut each day. By the time Friday afternoon arrived I had bid my working companion good-bye and he had wished me good luck on the following morning's project.

I pitched my tent about one-half mile from where this bird was doing his strutting and after a good supper, I set the clock to wake me at 4:00 A.M. and crawled into my sleeping bag. After fifteen minutes of tossing and turning while going over my hunting tactics for the next day, Morpheus beckoned and I slid into the land of dreams.

The sound of the clock brought me to the sitting position that I remained in for the next five minutes until I became almost awake. I crawled out of the tent and hit my head on the wing of the airplane. I have often wondered how a man who hates to rise as early as 4:00 A.M. could choose two things, his occupation and his passion, that both assure that he must arise at this ungodly hour each day.

Well, so be it. I made my coffee and ate my sweet rolls, washed my face once more, and dressed. I picked up the Martini and my call bag, then put on the insect repellent along with my hat and headed west along a dim trail that led to the end of this property. Just across the fence at the end of the air strip lay the gobbling ground of the fellow I had come there to rendezvous with. There was a scattering of palmettos all about the area, and I very quickly cut enough to build me a good blind.

I did not have to worry about taking the steps to keep from being shot by other hunters that I normally would have, as I knew for sure that I was the only one who had been given permission to hunt on this property. In the place I had built my blind the land slopped downhill slightly so I mounded a bit of sand in front of me to rest my rifle on. Lying on my stomach I stuck a few palmettos in a shape in front of me then placed a green cloth on the sand mound, and after checking my scope, I set my rifle on it. I listened and watched as little daylight eased into the pasture.

I hooted like an owl. No gobble. An owl answered me and I hooted several times in reply to his calling and in hopes of hearing a gobble as big daylight came on fast. The crows began their incessant calling close by but still there was no gobble from the old boy that I knew was on the limb, somewhere out there ahead of me about 150 yards away.

I looked at my watch and it was later than I thought. I picked up my slate and peg and cut loose two clucks and five yelps, given in a medium range, but still no sound from that end of the pasture. The sun rose bringing with it a fine morning. I yelped every fifteen or twenty minutes for the next two hours with never an answer.

The last time I looked at my watch it was almost 9:00 A.M. I clucked twice medium loud. As I set my slate aside I looked down the trail in front of me, and there came my bird, all puffed up and in full strut. His wattles were as red as a cherry, but despite his excitement, not a sound came from him. His presence was unnerving. One moment he was nowhere to be seen and the next moment it was as though he came as a vapor from the earth in front of me.

When he reached the forty yard mark, I put my cheek to the stock and the Redfield was filled with his presence. He came slowly and haltingly and I began my squeeze. At the moment I put the last bit of pressure on the trigger, this gobbler stepped into a depression in his path that dropped him almost a foot below my sight picture and the shot went above him. At once he became airborne and flew directly over my head and into a low hammock a quarter mile away in a southeasterly direction.

I waited twenty minutes and then walked along the fence line of the adjoining property. In a short time I reached the point where I felt the bird should be nearby and here I leaned against a fence post and clucked and purred on my slate once more. I received no answer from this silent bird but almost as soon as I had used the slate I caught a slight movement off to my right and then once more, this fine gobbler was standing before me forty yards away.

I rested my body against a hog wire fence with the rifle against a half grown gum tree. As he turned sideways to me, I placed the fourplex cross hairs on his wing butt and slowly squeezed the trigger. At the shot, he fell to the ground with a mighty thrashing of his wings and in a few seconds it was all over. I walked over and picked him up from where he had fallen in the ferns. He was a fine bird with a twelve-inch beard and one-and-a-half-inch spurs. He tipped the scales at nineteen and a quarter pounds.

We can only guess at the number of times this bird spread his wings in flight, but the flight in the baggage compartment of my aircraft, from Sarasota to our home in Williston was the last one he ever made. In the fall season of the late sixties. I made a hunt with an invitation from a friend named Reed Kempler. The property contained everything needed by sportsmen. There were deer in abundance, turkey, wild hogs, and small game that were plentiful at the time of my hunt. I doubt that there was any place in the state of Florida that contained the number and the quantity of all the species I have mentioned.

It was a huge tract of land running several miles long by perhaps four miles wide, extending all the way from Deer Park to the St. Johns River marsh on the eastern side of the property. As to a description of the land, I believe one might say that it contained almost every type of plant and soil that can be found in the state of Florida, with the possible exception of the Keys. It had royal palm, cabbage palm hammocks, high oak hammocks and low oak hammocks. These stood on marsh, swamp, large open flats of grass land, and large areas of open country covered with palmettos. In short, some of the finest game land to be found anywhere. Closer to the marsh on the southeast end of the ranch lay one of the most beautiful places I have ever seen or walked through in my lifetime.

The area I speak of contained perhaps fifty acres, but Lord what a fifty acres. It was hip boot country going in as I had to wade from one small hammock to another in wet times until I reached this spot. However, when I reached it I forgot all of the rough time I had getting there, because as I stood there looking at the entrance to this plateau, overwhelmed, for there before me lay one of the most beautiful groves of mature royal palm trees left in the state. I would not hazard a guess as to the age of this stand of palms, but I have been told that they are well over 100 years old. In looking at the size of them and their condition, I am sure that they were every bit of that. I can say with certainty that each time I sat in this hammock with the first rays of a chilly winter sunrise spilling through the tree tops into the mist rising from the floor of the hammock, it gave me a feeling of serenity and a sense of having had a sneak preview of paradise. I always came away from this place with a profound feeling almost as though I had reached out and touched the face of God.

I recall a hunt made there in mid December of 1969. I had been invited by Reed Kempler to come to the ranch for a weekend hunt. I drove to Deer Park, met with Reed, and was told that because some of the cattle had broken loose and had to be rounded up, he would not be able to hunt with me on this trip. I was told that I could hunt the southeast portion of the ranch and that I could make camp by myself on the south end, if I cared too. I have camped quite a bit by myself and don't mind it greatly, but given a preference, I like to have a companion to sit around a campfire with. However, as always in life we have to play the game with the cards we have been dealt.

I drove to the southeast end and after setting up camp, I put on my hip boots, put my rifle on my shoulder, and headed north along the dim trail that lead to the royal palm hammock. December had been dry so the going was not too rough. About halfway through the section that led to the palm hammock, I scattered a drive of hogs and they in turn scattered a bedded group of eight or ten deer that I could catch only an occasional glimpse of as they ran west through the dense stands of cabbage palm, which grew profusely everywhere to my left side in the small, wet hammock that I was passing through. I eased along now at a slower pace, upset with myself for spooking the hogs.

I have always had to fight the impulse to hurry through the woods to the place I intend to make my hunt. With the full knowledge that this is wrong due to the number of animals I have spooked and lost throughout a lifetime of hunting, I still must, from time to time, tell myself to slow down and look back and from side to side as I head to my place of all places where the big one will be waiting for me. As I get older, I find many times that in going a bit slower, I often kill the big one before I reach my place of places. I have written in another chapter of this impulse to hurry but feel that it is important enough to say once more. In game country the hunt starts when you close your vehicle door.

As I approached the place I intended to hunt, I looked at my watch and saw that it would soon be 3:00 P.M. I stepped into the hammock and was amazed at the carpet of grass growing there. It looked in every respect like a well-kept golf course. Cattle grazed there throughout the year and due to the number of palm trees, full sunlight was shaded out to a great extent. The grass there was never higher than four inches any time I ever saw it. I began to look for turkey sign and had no trouble in finding it. The bulk of the activity seemed to be centered at the west end of the flat where several large oaks were dropping acorns. After walking around a bit, I decided to set up by the side of one of the oaks, facing west by northwest and after checking the outside of my blind, I was not pleased until I had added a few more palm fronds to it. I sat down inside and was quite pleased with the setup.

I checked my rifle and shells, took a sip of water from my canteen, put my back against the oak, relaxed, and sat back to await developments. Twenty minutes after cleaning the surface and peg, I clucked, purred, and gave five or six yelps. After a wait of five minutes, I did the same series of calls once more. I received the same results for my efforts as I had on my first calls.

The afternoon wore on without a great deal to excite a turkey hunter. I knew that turkeys had been there the day before as I had found many fresh dusting mounds and in the dry places, ample droppings, scratchings, and enough preened feathers to suggest two flocks of turkeys were using the area each day. I called time and again at twenty-minute intervals, but all I could pick up was the calling of crows in the distance, the drumming of woodpeckers, and now and again the loud cry of the Lord God, the name given the piliated woodpecker by old time native Floridians.

I watched and marveled at the number of gray squirrels racing around the oaks before me and noticed that the shadows were getting longer and that the sun was setting lower in the west. I reached into my call bag and pulled out one of my pill boxes. When I opened the lid, I knew I had the medicine I needed. I reached into the box and took out Penns woods mouth yelper, let it soak for a minute or so and cut loose with a nine or ten-note kee-kee run with three loud yelps tacked on the end. I received an answer almost as soon as I called. I shot another kee-kee run with five or six yelps on the end and received another call that was made closer to my blind than the last one. I picked up my slate and peg and gave a series of soft pit-pit calls ending in two medium clucks and some purring. This turkey, and I did not know whether it was a hen or gobbler—was now within fifty yards of me, but would not, for the time being, expose itself.

The shadows were long now, and dusk was not far away. The situation had me in a bit of a bind. I did not want to shoot a hen and in a very short time I would be unable to distinguish the sex of the bird if it stepped out. So once more I picked up the slate and clucked low twice. At this the turkey stepped out of ti-tis and gallberry bushes at the back end of the flat. I looked through the scope, and very quickly saw that this bird was a two-year-old, a young gobbler with a five-inch beard. He did not give me any time to deal with him though. Almost as soon as he stepped out he began a brisk walk through some ferns, nervously feeding as he walked along until he was hidden from my view entirely by bushes at the edge of a small partly dried up cypress pond.

A brown thrasher began to play around the base of the tree next to my blind, scratching at this and that.

Watching this bird made me recall the words of Sam Poore, my wife's uncle and mine by marriage. Sam said, "When the thrasher begins to play around your blind, the turkeys are already on the limb." When it came to turkey hunting and you wanted to learn something, you had better listen because he did not talk much, but when Sam told you something it was always the pure quill.

As I watched first the thrasher and then the last spot where I had seen the turkey, I found myself hoping both birds were a little off schedule. I had begun to think that this gobbler had trotted north, which was the direction he came from, and would roost 500 yards or so, somewhere in that direction. This thought had hardly passed when with a great flapping of wings, this solitary bird flew to roost in a cypress tree about eighty yards west of me. He changed limbs twice and at landing on this second limb he shifted around until he was pleased with his position.

Until he flew up, this bird had without making a sound remained at a spot not fifteen feet away from where I had last seen him. I had thought that he might be joined there by others of his flock, but he was not. I let him get settled down for the night and looking through the scope I could yet make out his beard in the remaining light. I was not pleased at this eighty-yard offhand shot with so little light to shoot by. I slowly eased out of the back of my blind and found a small gum tree I could lean the rifle against. The bird showed no sign of being uneasy or having seen or heard my change of position from the blind to the gum tree. I eased the rifle around the little tree until I found the picture that I wanted. With the very last rays of a winter sun, I placed the cross hairs at the apex of this bird's pulley bone and squeezed off the shot. I watched him tumble end over end, as he fell earthward from a perch from where I am sure he had seen the sun go down many times before. I walked to the base of the tree where the bird had fallen and paced off seventy yards. As I did so I took my eyes off of this cypress. Let me inject here that the rule in dove hunting of never taking your eyes off of the spot where the dove falls also holds true for turkeys shot in a dried up cypress pond near dark. I had no flashlight and it was black dark before I found this bird. He was ten more yards behind the tree I believed him to be lying under. He was a fine bird, weighing seventeen pounds with a five-inch beard, one-inch long spurs, and acorn fat.

The night sounds as I worked my way back south to my camp were music to my ears. Hogs and deer were feeding everywhere. Many deer blew at me as I walked along, I could hear hogs feeding and the squeal of one hog being bitten by another. Owls, herons, and limpkins joined the night song, all adding to a picture that is as fresh in my mind as if it had taken place yesterday.

The two hunts in the first part of this chapter covered shots made at short and medium ranges. Now I will tell you of one or two hunts in which I made very long shots, very long indeed, at very big gobblers. I had been given an assignment by our office in Lakeland, Florida to spray a series of canals that had become completely blocked by water hyacinths. They were preventing boat travel in the area around and into the main canal leading into Blue Cypress lake, a lake noted for its excellent bass and crappie fishing. The lake lies west of the city of Vero Beach and was at the time I write of, surrounded by marshland and cattle pasture. Some of the cattlemen had turned a large amount of land into improved pasture, but most of the land around the lake was wild, unimproved pasture. I will say that in the early and mid-sixties this county was all that a sportsman could ask for. You could not have ordered a better place to fish and hunt from the Sears Roebuck catalog. Deer, turkey, wild hogs, quail, ducks, and all manner of small game abounded in the area as did many fur-bearing species. If you were a fisherman the door was open wide.

There were cabins for rent and boats were also available if you did not have one in tow. As to hunting in the area, unless you knew one of the ranchers well, you would have to make yourself content with watching the number of turkeys, deer, and hogs that were sure to be feeding early and late along the only road leading into McIntire's fish camp, as the only shooting you could do and stay out of jail was with a thirty-five-millimeter camera and a telephoto lens. The ranchers in the area around the lake would, however, allow hunting by friends, family, and a few people that had trapped and caught frogs for a living all of their lives in this area and were known to all thereabouts. Some of the old trappers had no home but lived out of their boats, which they covered by a tarp or a tent pitched by the lakeside canal bank or an island.

I recall well an old fellow who came on occasion to visit with us when he knew that several of us had rented the log house. This cabin was built over water, on stilts and with a fine fishing deck attached. We always rented this cabin in advance as it would sleep eight men and had full cooking facilities. Logging camps, fire departments, telephone line crews in wilderness areas, game wardens, and any number of other occupations where men are without benefit of the hand that rocks the cradle always had two or three men who become good cooks over the years. And so it was at our house on stilts at Blue Cypress Lake.

We lived well. I might almost say in high style most of the time. Of the six to eight men who stayed there, four of us could cook as well as most women, and two could cook better than most. It suffices to say that no one ever lost weight during the month long period or more that we were there each time. On the night that I write of, our table was graced by the presence of an old man who had been a cowboy when all of Florida was an open range that contained wild scrub cattle that sometimes never saw a horse and rider for two years at a time. The old time Florida scrub cow was small and tough. He could get by on nothing and had to. The old time Florida range cow never saw a bale of hay, a molasses supplement, or a mineral block. It was root, hog or die, and many of the older cattle never made it through a hard winter. When penned up with no way out, this breed of cow would attack both horse and rider. A man on a good horse could get away but a man on foot was in a bad predicament. It was much like the Spanish bull ring. This kind of life was all this old man had known from the time he was able to sit in a saddle and do a man's work, until the coming of the Model T Ford and the new Florida that was developing.

Real estate was booming and the influx of new people and new money created opportunities no one had dreamed of. The sale of frog legs was one of these. The young cowboy, back from fighting the war to end all wars, had a little mustering-out pay he had saved. He knew he could catch enough frogs from the Felsmere marsh to supply the restaurants in West Palm Beach and Miami if he could devise a boat that could run through the weeds in the shallow water without burning up the motor. He gave much thought to this and came up with the idea of building a welded framework inside the boat and mounting an overhauled Model T engine with an airplane propeller pushing backward. He put it together and in doing so created one of the first airboats, and frogged and trapped fur-bearing animals in the Felsmere Marsh for most of his lifetime. He was a man in his seventies I would guess. Somewhat arthritic, I would say from exposure to the elements, but other than that, he seemed to be enjoying good health.

Uncle Willie Giger, had cooked lima beans with several hamhocks and baked hot biscuits and corn bread. He also made a big pot of collard greens and a big tossed salad, and Henry Willison had made a huge tray of vanilla pudding with vanilla wafers. After giving thanks for this bounty, we told our guest to help himself and this he did, *con gusto!* I don't believe that I ever saw a small man eat that much before. The fun came when all had taken a helping of vanilla pudding and then passed the tray, which was half-full at this point, to our guest. He took his spoon and raked the entire half that was left into his plate with the statement that of all things on earth to eat, this was his favorite and that it was hard for him to stop as he got to taste it so infrequently. I think we all were pleased to see this old fellow enjoy himself. The table he sat down to most of the time was like Mother Hubbard's cupboard. Afterward, we lit our pipes and as I recall we had a dram or two as he told us many strange, humorous, interesting, and wonderful tales of a Florida that had mostly vanished almost thirty years before. All who sat around this old man listening to him relate one experience after another soon began to see, through his eyes, the enormity of the paradise lost.

He told us of the days when a man could ride a horse from the north side of Lake Okeechobee all the way to Tampa, unencumbered, and as evening time came on, the people in any dwelling he rode by would ask him to get down and take supper and spend the night. Pond birds were in numbers uncountable. Before the tick eradication program was put into effect by the cattlemen, deer were everywhere as were wild turkeys, and while most hogs bore the ear mark of the owner, there were always some unmarked hogs in the marsh that could be classified as wild and could be had for the taking. One just had to leave the ears on the hide when skinning it so the owner of the hogs that it was running with would not think you were skinning one of his. That evening was one of the most enjoyable that I have ever passed, anywhere and at any time. We all bid the old gent good night, and I thanked him for sharing his experiences with us. He in turn thanked us for the meal and expressed the wish that he could eat the vanilla wafer banana pudding every day of the week. I told him that if he would drop by at noontime one day he could take lunch with us and I would make him a peach cobbler so good that he would shove his grandmother in the creek to get the last bite left in the bowl.

He came one more time about three weeks later and sat down to both dinner and supper with us, and true to my word, I made him a cobbler. When he finished the evening meal and we asked him if he would eat more, he said, "No, I have had a bait of everything. No, come to think of it I've had a gorge." We were treated once more to hunting and fishing tales, both fresh and salt water, and the evening ended with one of the best laughs we all had in a long time. As I related before, this old gent was an old time trapper and had made perhaps a third of his livelihood from the sale of gator hides, and coon and otter skins most of his adult life.

He told us, "Boys, I don't know what I am going to do. They have put gators on the protected list. Frogging in Felsmere Marsh has gone to hell with so many airboats out there it looks like downtown West Palm Beach after dark. Boys, I trapped over three hundred and fifty otters in the lake and the canals around it last year and now I have trapped all season long and can hardly catch an otter. I don't know what in hell has happened to all of the otters in this area. It used to be as good a place to catch otters as a man could want. I guess some kind of otter sickness has got into them and they all died off." At this point in his tale of woe most of us were having a hard time suppressing our laughter. I believe it was Les Libby, one of our crew, who suggested that 350 otters were perhaps, a large number of animals to remove from an area this size without depleting the breeding stock for two or three seasons.

At this remark, the old man grinned and said, "Well, that just might be because if I know anything, know how to catch an otter and perhaps I had hit it a wee bit too hard in the area around the lake." He thanked us for the fine meal and then did something he had never done before. He turned and thanked us for our company, bid us good night and stepped through the door to oblivion. I never saw him again, except in a few dreams I had, and in the many times, over the years with my head on the pillow, I summoned up his presence to hear once more the tales of an Eden unspoiled as yet by the hands of man.

It was a short time after the old gentleman left that I made friends with Jack Holman, caretaker and brother of Bud Holman, the man who owned the ranch and airstrip that we were conducting our spray operations from. The Holman ranch was located at the very southwest end of Blue Cypress Lake and had a twelve-foot dike that encompassed the entire ranch. I do not recall the number of acres there but it was a sizable ranch with the advantage of a fine, well-kept, sod landing strip that had multiengine aircraft capabilities. On any flight that I made from this strip in the twenty-three years I flew for the Florida Game and Fresh Water Fish Commission, I was almost certain to see game of some sort there or on the ranches that butted up to the Holman property.

Anyway, a long time coworker, friend, and hunting companion, Rex Land was working out of his usual slot as supervisor and was acting as my loader, putting chemicals into the aircraft from the tank truck. It was springtime and the legal turkey gobbling season had been in effect for over two weeks, and as we were wiping the dew away from the windscreen, and gas and chemical gages, we could hear several turkeys gobbling south of the airstrip. We filled the plane with chemical and I flew out with the first load of the morning.

The canal I was spraying was some fifteen minutes away, and because it was a long, straight run down the canal it took a matter of ten minutes and I was on my way back to the strip. As I swung over the south end of the strip I saw a sight to gladden the heart of any nature lover, bird watcher, and let us not leave out the turkey hunter. Below the wings of my aircraft, off to my left, I could see about 50 turkeys. This is not unusual in this section of Florida as many of the sod farms and the Mormon ranch north of this location have flocks of 80 and 100 turkeys feeding in one large open pasture from time to time, however, the fact that one gobbler had thirty-eight hens hemmed up and was holding off ten other gobblers, four mature and six jakes, was unusual. He was servicing the hens and strutting back and forth in front of the gobblers. As I pulled to one side and watched this show for five minutes or so he serviced two hens.

I landed and told my compadre what I had seen and to go back to the cabin and get my little 218. As I had already obtained permission for us to hunt there, he could kill one of the gobblers while I was off with the next load. Rex would hear nothing of this and said that he would wait till I got back and if the morning wind had reached a velocity of more than eight miles per hour, we would both go together as our spraying would be over due to the chemical we were using and the drift factor. At this point we had never had a major lawsuit due to crop damage caused by our spray judgment. Watching the drift factors kept us out of the courtroom.

As I recall I delivered three more loads before the wind got up. Each time I checked on this old boy he was still holding the other gobblers at bay and still doing his thing. I could only shake my head in disbelief, thirty-eight in one morning! I guess the word *boss gobbler* and everything the word implies could be given to this fellow. I have seen gobblers with fifteen or twenty hens in South Florida or so but thirty-eight is unheard of. Six to eight hens and even less is normal for one gobbler in the area of the state I live in, the central region.

As I was coming in from spraying the last load, I circled the south end of the strip and I could see that the old fellow had worked his way through the bunch, to the point that he only had about fifteen left to contend with and some of his competition had gone back into the woods. I saw two mature gobblers and two jakes. I landed and as Rex and I tied the aircraft down, I told him what I had just seen on the way in. He in turn told me that the wind had began to rise twenty minutes after I had taken off and he had gone back to camp, picked up the 218B, and told Jack Holman we were going to try to shoot a gobbler. We started along the top of the canal bank at a dog trot as I knew that the birds would soon leave the pasture and go into the woods on the other side of the canal.

We kept up this pace as long as a forty-five-year-old man could, then dropped down to a brisk walk that soon put us to within 300 yards of the birds. I told Rex to take the 218 and kill a gobbler but he would not so I eased down the side of the dike and walked east about 100 yards. I slowly stuck my head above the top of the dike and with my binoculars began to search the area for the turkeys. I glassed the area at the point where I had last seen all of the birds together and for some reason, I could not see one bird anywhere. I came back down and told Rex that the turkeys had left the area and had gone into the swamp. He thought perhaps not and taking the binoculars he went topside for a look. He caught a movement in some small oaks farther east of our position, and we knew we had not walked far enough down the dike. We hustled on the backside of the dike to a point we thought would bring us abreast of the birds, and once more the rifle was offered and refused. I wiggled up the back side and peeked over the top and sure enough there they were. Only a handful now though. The old boy was still in full strut and dropped it only to service one of the four hens he had left. The mature gobblers had left the field of battle and only the two jakes remained to receive instruction.

I looked through the Redfield and waited for him to finish his courtship. As he shook out his feathers and tightened them up again, I put the cross hairs on his wing butts and touched one off. The five other turkeys flew south across our heads into the pines and ti-tis across the canal. I looked at the old warrior lying on the ground eighty yards before me and felt a pang of remorse. The gobbler was one of the best I have ever taken and while we were unable to weigh him before removing his intestines he still tipped the scales at twenty-one pounds and had a full eleven-inch beard and curved one-and-a-half-inch spurs.

I made two other hunts on the Holman ranch and they were both successful but I shall only tell of one. This hunt was made at the tail end of the gobbling season in which I killed the fellow with thirty-eight sweethearts. I had told my wife that I intended to spend the night at Holman's camp and hunt the next morning then fly home that afternoon. The alarm clock in Jack's bedroom woke me from a sound sleep in the next room. I got up and looked at the clock and it was 4:30 A.M. We put the coffee pot on and as it began to rattle the lid, the aroma became overwhelming. After our second cup and two eggs over light with bacon, grits, and toast with homemade grape jelly, we began to feel like real men should. I asked Jack if he was going to go with me to the flat where the gobbler was. He replied in the negative, stating that he had to work on a transfer pump and might have to go get parts. I took one more cup of coffee and bade him a fond *adieu* and headed southeast to the flat the gobbler had been using all week long. After about thirty minutes of walking I came to the area I had in mind. The grass in this part of the pasture was cropped very close and as I stepped out on the flat six turkeys stepped out also.

I was in a bind. There was a small tree that forked right at chest height somewhat like a boy's slingshot. This tree and the distance to the turkeys was the only thing that had kept them standing there. Had I been closer, they would have run back into the fringe of palmettos as soon as they saw me. The distance was awesome! I looked through my binoculars and could see a good gobbler and five hens, all standing like statues, necks craned as tall as they could reach. I placed an elbow on each branch of the tree formed by the "Y" and it made for a perfect rest. As it was just good daylight, the wind was flat calm. I put the cross hairs on the gobbler's neck, then knowing my bullet drop I put the cross hairs at the top of the gobbler's head for a thirteen-inch inch drop. The sound of the shot seemed to bounce back and forth off of the canal bank and all of the turkeys became airborne. I said to myself, "Good try, old boy, but just a wee bit too far." Then I told myself, "Hey, wait just a minute that was a good rest, a good squeeze, a good picture, go check it out." I paced off the steps from the tree I had rested on to make the shot and when I arrived at the spot where the turkeys had been standing I had paced off 273 long steps. I might add that lying there before me was a dandy gobbler killed so dead he did not even flounce. He merely spread his wings and fell forward. The five hens were nesting somewhere close by as this was very late in the spring season. In all probability they each had most of their eggs in the nest at the time this gobbler was killed.

This was the longest shot, by far, that I had ever made with a turkey rifle. Most of what I had called long range, and still do, would fall into the 100- to 150-yard class, easy shots for the 218B if you take your time from a good rest. I doubt very seriously that I would even entertain the thought of a shot at this range today. The 218B would be equal to the occasion but I don't feel that I would be. I was twenty years younger than I am now and a much better rifle shot then.

The bird came from a gene pool that produced some wonderfully strong and healthy birds. It was another fine, mature gobbler weighing eighteen pounds and having long, keen spurs and an eleven-inch beard. So ended a good morning hunt in a beautiful place.

Love Affair with a Sixty-five-year-old Gal

I have often pondered this question: Is having a friend who owns a gun shop and sporting goods store a blessing or a curse? I should know the answer to this by now. As twice in a span of forty years I have been in the position to weigh this question in the balance; once as a young man and again as an old one. However, at this point, the jury is still out, yet I get the uncomfortable feeling that I have very little moral restraint when I hear the words "Take it on home with you this weekend and see how it shoots, it seems to fit you." I put it to my shoulder and it feels so good. The children can be without milk, the lady of the house wearing dresses that are five years old, the family auto looks like one of Henry Ford's first efforts, and the mortgage on the family castle due next week, but when the man says, "You know, you don't have to pay for this all at once; we can make it like you want it."—of such words are addictions born.

I walked into the gun shop of a friend of mine one day in the spring of 1989 and saw that he had a twelve-gauge Ansley Fox, double-barrel shotgun sitting in a section of the shop that was generally reserved for guns brought in for repair. I asked if it was in for repair and he stated that he had picked the gun up in a trade at a gun show in Orlando, Florida, and that although it was sitting in the repair department, it was only there because it had not been priced and inventoried yet. I picked it up and put it to my shoulder and looked down the barrels and it fit like a glove. It was an old gun, made about 1925, well within the period of time known as the golden age of gun making in this country. The gun had been used, to be sure, but it had not been misused and when it was breached then locked again it was as tight as a new gun. I put it back in the rack, talked a bit with my compadre behind the counter, and eased on up the road to my castle.

When I got home I hugged my wife and lifted the lids on all of the pots on the stove. After dinner I sat back and relaxed in the recliner as visions of sugar plums danced through my head. What a fine old gun and in such splendid shape for having been around so long. After that day I gave it only an occasional thought until I walked back into the store a month and a half later and there sat the Ansley Fox still on the rack. When I asked why it was still around I was told it had been to three gun shows since I had put it to my shoulder and at one show it carried only a $275.00 price tag and still it went begging. I picked it up once more and looked through the barrels, they were mirror bright. We checked the constriction of both chokes and they gauged full and full, a turkey hunter's delight. The balance and feel of a high-grade double-barrel gun has always had an appeal for me that I find lacking in other types of shotguns. I have killed many turkeys with pump guns and over and unders but I started my wing shooting career with a high grade side-by-side and I still find that I am best suited by this type of gun.

We talked a bit more about this fine old piece and after much bickering, a custom skinning knife, a small hand ax made by Marble in the thirties, a two-bladed trapper pocket knife, and a wee bit of folding money changed hands. I took this old sweetheart to the house. I had time before sundown to grab a handful of short magnum shells in a mixture of shot sizes, some in the old style shells and also some of the new Remington duplex loads 2 × 6, 2 × 4, 4 × 6, and headed for the woods to see how it would shoot. I knew how well the new duplex loads worked on both the patterning board and on turkeys when shot from a 870 wing master pump but wanted to know how this old fox would handle these new duplex loads.

After a trip to the field, I came back as pleased as punch with this old fossil. I found the left tube to be choked slightly tighter than the right and when tested at ranges of ten to sixty yards, this barrel consistently put more shot into the head and neck area of the side view of a turkey target. The right barrel marked full also was not far behind in tight patterning but it brings us back to the fact that the choke designation stamped on the barrel only gives part of the story. Testing it with different loads will give us the rest.

The drawing of a turkey head and neck thirteen inches long that was set up at fifty yards, showed nine hits in the head and neck, shot from the left-hand barrel with the four-by-six Remington duplex load. The right barrel gave five hits in the same area with the same load. I shot three more rounds of this load through both barrels and at the same range. After counting the pellets in the head and neck area of all targets, I found no less than five hits and had up to thirteen on one.

I felt that I was ready to go to the turkey woods. I did have one other refinement in mind. Something I like on any shotgun that I shoot. I had the stock cut and a high grade pachmyer skeet size recoil pad installed bringing the length of pull to fourteen and a quarter inches. The short magnum shells have considerable back thrust after shooting fifteen or twenty rounds at a patterning board and without a recoil pad installed. I tend to feel as though I have gone three rounds with Sonny Liston.

The gobbling season was only three weeks away when the work on the stock was completed and only another turkey hunter could understand how long that three weeks can be but I was ready. I might say more than ready and yet there is always the ritual of the calls. We go through our call bag bringing out this wing bone given by a friend, this one that we made twenty-five years ago, the slate and peg that has given forty years of yeoman's service and put many a fine turkey on the carrying strap or the box calls, most without names, bought when I was a young man from old men that made them in backyard woodsheds, some of them very good indeed. All must be played with, touched, fondled, yelped, clucked, kee-keed, chalked, and yelped again ad infinitum.

Some of this is practice but much of this is ritual and is as perennial as the white blossoms of the dogwood at this time of season. A lot of hard practice takes place at this time and most of it should have been ongoing throughout the year. What great musician who has ever lived let a full season pass without touching his instrument? The fact that many hunters go from season to season without using the calls they have, makes hunting turkeys a lot more easy for the guys that do call well. This is not to say that calling is everything, it is not. Woodsmanship counts more or at least as much but it does increase your success ratio if you are good with the calls you use.

I checked over all of my hunting gear and started putting each thing in its proper place. I had bought a new ten-by-six camo net blind. A piece of equipment I feel that is almost as essential as my gun and I had not yet cut the shooting port holes in this net, so this was done and a nylon parachute cord twenty-five feet long was attached to the top side of the net. This length cord will get you by in most areas. As you will find something you can tie your blind fast to. I put my compass, bug dope, garden shears, camo poncho, extra cord, extra knife, and a small pint plastic bottle of water in the bag attached to the bottom of my shooting stool. I take a lot of ribbing about the things I carry but you can't go back and get it once they start gobbling and you are in your blind.

The weekend before the opening of the gobbling season I called my hunting companion Jack Van Dervort and suggested that we ease on out to check on a place called Turkey Island on the west side of the Withlacoochee River off Highway 200 between Ocala and Hernando, Florida.

Turkey Island was not given that name because a family named Turkey had homesteaded it in years past. It has now and as far back as most of the old timers can remember always had a good resident and also a good transient population of turkeys. After walking through this property, a person able to recognize what constitutes a good turkey habitat will understand how the island derived its name. A grove of one-hundred-year-old live oak trees cover parts of the island with open grass flats growing underneath their moss laden canopy. Cypress ponds and cypress swamps lie to the east of the island and run all the way to the Withlacoochee River. The property has many water oaks, turkey oaks, live oaks, sweet gums, red maples, and patches of broom sedge. Some of the open flats made it very easy for a hen that is grass hoppering with her poults to run a few steps and vanish from harm's way. A vast tract of uninhabited land that contained much of the same type of terrain lay to the south of this property ran for miles and was also fronted by the river.

This property has always been fine game country and has changed little in the forty years that I have known it.

In the fifties through the seventies the property always had many wild turkeys, a large number of feral hogs, and a few deer. In the early- and mid-1950s this area always had a large winter population of green head mallards, teal, gadwalls, and pintail ducks but this was lost to us in recent years due to the farming practices in some of our northern states, natural changes in the northern breeding areas, and in some of the land use on and surrounding some of our U.S. wildlife refuges. Except for the wood ducks that are in the area on a year-around basis and the few diving ducks that come in the winter, there is hardly any reason for anyone to put out a set of decoys.

On the morning that my compadre and I checked out Turkey Island just one week ahead of the gobbling season, we were more than pleased with the signs that we found in abundance at each of the areas where we normally set up our blinds. In the sand roads leading to our hunt areas we found gobbler tracks and hen tracks. Strutting signs were in the trail where the gobblers had left drag marks with their wing tips while they strutted in tight circles around the hens. The droppings of both sexes were everywhere along with feathers that had been lost in preening. The end of one road led back into a small field and in this field we found over ten dusting mounds, all in daily use for the past week. The length of this road was bordered on its east side by a vast cypress swamp dry for the past two seasons due to a short term drought and low water conditions on the river. After looking at each section of the island, we were ready to open the season that afternoon but we thought we could contain our excitement for six more days so we eased on out of this little part of paradise and drove to the house.

The clock jarred me into something that would have to pass for consciousness at 3:30 A.M. and as always I did not want to get up. I had to tell myself that it was the opening day of the 1990 gobbling season and that I had to pick up a fellow named Jack Van Dervort at 4:30 A.M. in front of his house. As always cold water on the back of the neck and hot coffee sipped at short intervals can bring about a remarkable transformation. Within fifteen minutes I was almost human. I have a very good friend, who incidentally does not hunt, who one time asked me how in heavens name could anyone get up at such an ungodly hour to go into the woods before daylight, stumbling over cypress knees, with insects of all kinds constantly biting you, being wet from the waist down, and uncomfortable from every stand point, and still say this was an enjoyable experience instead of some form of madness. I recall telling him some foolishness about only the anointed would understand or some other esoteric nonsense, knowing in my heart that he was at least half right. Turkey hunting is a form of madness. A sweet madness to be sure but madness most certainly.

I finished my second cup of coffee and had my bowl of hot cereal. Dressed and picked up the Ansley Fox and got into the Bronco. Jack was ready and waiting outside when I pulled up in front of his house. We put his gun, a Browning over-and-under twelve-gage and the rest of his gear into the Bronco and headed out on the road to the place where all cares and worries are forgotten, or if not forgotten put on hold. We drove to the home of the man who looked after the farm and blinked our lights twice, to let him know that we were on the property. After doing this we turned out of his yard and rolled onto a narrow sand road that ran east to Turkey Island. I cut our lights as we entered the west side of the island but had to turn them back on low beam once more as my night vision would not permit me to drive through the hammock with the existing light.

The road through the hammock was tight, very tight in many places. A lot of almost hairpin turns exist on this trail as you travel the first half of it. I swore to myself and to my partner that not many moons would pass before a pair of workable war surplus blackout lights would adorn the grill of the Bronco.

The turkeys that we were to hunt were roosted in the big cypress swamp to the east of us and while it is thick in the swamp and the possibility of a roosting turkey picking up the reflection of the lights from an incoming vehicle is somewhat remote, this is just another variable that could change the end result of a hunt. Thirty years ago headlight beams and trucks and cars rattling through the woods made little difference to roosting gobblers. You could even slam a car door and if a gobbler was roosted near by he might even gobble but alas those days slipped away along with good five-cent cigars, ten-cent coca-cola and thirty-five cent hamburgers dressed all the way.

We have a smarter bird now. He is less prone to gobble than the turkey of thirty years ago. This is not to say that many of the second year toms will not start gobbling at first light and keep it up til 8:30. They will. I had one gobbler eighty-two times this season. I knew that this one was going home with me. It seemed that when I would cluck a time or two and follow it with five or six fast yelps on my wing bone that this bird would double gobble before I could give my last yelp.

He would walk through the cypress swamp east of me to a point about 200 yards from my blind and there he would stop and gobble and gobble and gobble. Exciting? You bet, but also maddening! This bird would strut and gobble then turn and head east toward the river. He would almost go out of hearing and then in answer to a series of calls on the wing bone, he would gobble, reverse his line of travel, and head back west to a point 100 or 200 yards away from my position. There he would start and go through his new found mating urge once more. Did I say at the start of this that I knew I was going to put him on my turkey strap? Well, I believe that I did eventually but it sure didn't happen on this occasion.

On the morning that I write of, this two-year-old bird emerged as the victor in this little game we were playing. This fellow, after two and a half hours of hard play, made the last move that checkmated me. When he turned back east and started his slow amble to the river, gobbling as he went, I had no more moves left on the board. This two-year-old was acting like a five-year-old with the exception of the great number of calls he made. I find the older birds nowadays, the fellows with the ten- and twelve-inch beards are not overly talkative; five or six gobbles at first light then maybe a few gobbles a little bit later as he comes to your calling and might even come right up to your blind without giving so much as a cluck until he is standing in back of it looking at you before he runs or flies.

As my old friend Jack Carter of Fairfield, Florida, now departed, once said of one of his father's Walker Fox hounds: "He has a fine voice but you never get to hear much of it in a chase, because he is so stingy mouthed." Many old gobblers are now like that very stingy mouthed. But to return to Turkey Island and this season's opening day.

We pulled up to the new hog pen trap at the west edge of the cypress swamp and found the pickup truck belonging to Mr. John Quincy Adams, better known as

Quincy to the folks here about. Quincy is now seventy-two years old and has hunted this area since he was big enough to carry a gun. He is one of the best turkey hunters I have ever known and I might add that he will normally kill two birds with every three shells in a dove field, and I have seen him run ten and twelve straight in a good dove field on a good day without missing. When he is out of earshot we call him our national treasure but we would never let him hear this as he is hard enough to live with already.

When Jack and I saw Quincy's truck at the hog pen, we knew that our plans had been altered. Dust mounds would by rights be turned over to Mr. Quincy this morning. Jack and I had hunted the area two years in a row on opening day, so we didn't feel too badly about relinquishing this spot with all of the strutting signs, droppings, and preened feathers. Another way to look at this is that any man, seventy-two years old, who will get up at 3:00 A.M. everyday of the gobbling season to greet the new dawn is due at least this much respect. There are only so many turkey seasons in the bag for all of us and at seventy-two who knows how many are left.

We tapped on the window of the pickup truck and Quincy woke up. We drank coffee, talked a bit, and told him where we were going to set up south of him one-half mile. We drove to the south boundary line and set Jack up in his blind in a spot where two gobblers had strutted the day before and several hens were making a daily promenade back and forth. Seeing that he was set in all respects, I beat a hasty retreat to a point almost a mile north of his position and 300 yards east into the cypress swamp. First light was twenty minutes past as I hurried to set up my blind much later than I normally would, but on this day it couldn't be helped.

I settled down relaxed a bit and pulled out my wing bone. I clucked about four times, not fast, with seconds between each cluck then I hit an eight-note series of yelps and in reply I heard nothing. I let five minutes pass and repeated the same sequence of calls and received the same response. I called on the wing bone giving both clucks and yelps three times in the next ten minutes.

A short interval of time had elapsed from my last call when a shotgun was fired one time north of my position. Unless I had miscoursed the sound of the shot it could have came only from the area in use by Mr. John Quincy Adams. I remained in my blind for ten minutes and then I started out of the swamp. About halfway out I heard a pickup truck engine come to life and by the time I reached the hog trap Mr. Q had left the hunt area. As it had worked out Quincy had called up and killed a fine nineteen-pound gobbler with a ten-inch beard. I had never heard the bird gobble but then it was very thick in the swamp and with spring foliage on all of the trees, sound does not carry very far. The leaves on all of the low bushes and trees act as a sound baffle.

I went south to the blind I had left my partner in and he said he had yelped and clucked on his slate ten minutes before we heard Quincy shoot and had a hen and a big gobbler came out to the road through the thicket. As he turned to look at the movement he had seen out of the corner of his eye, the gobbler stepped back into the thicket. The hen stood there on the outside edge of the road for thirty seconds before following the gobbler to his date with destiny. Walking swiftly to the point where Quincy sat in his blind with his magic slate and peg, ten minutes later the gobbler had greeted his last sunrise.

Jack and I stretched our legs, talked a bit and headed down the road to the area that the shot had come from.

We found Quincy's blind and the fired shell in the place where the noble bird was standing that last fatal second. I had brought a rolled-up blind with me, so we set up to give it a try. Jack said he could hear another bird gobbling at the same time Quincy was working his bird. This turkey was southeast of the bird Quincy was calling. So I thought we might be looked on favorably by the gods, yet.

We settled in and got all of the leaves and limbs from underfoot, wanting no noise at the wrong moment. I sat back, pulled out the wing bone, and cut loose. I had an answer within a second. Not a gobbler but a turkey to be sure. I clucked fairly loudly and then yelped about six times. The birds were coming and two of them were talking to me. They were northeast of us in the swamp but getting closer with each call I made. The next yelps made by the turkeys let me know they were getting very close. I put the wing bone away at this point and took out the slate and peg. Took a sip of water from my small bottle because for some reason my mouth had become very dry and then placed a diaphragm call in the roof of my mouth, put the Ansley Fox across my knees, and prepared to do business.

As it so happened we did not have long to wait. I had just given a series of low yelps followed by medium range clucking and purring. Suddenly four adult hens filed through an opening in front of us at a distance of about forty yards. Then what we both took to be a young gobbler with a four-inch beard ran in and began to herd the hens together, and then we lost them all in the thicket that edged the swamp. We could never have taken a shot at the one bird that we both believed to be a jake due to the thickness of the foliage. To have taken the shot at this turkey would have more than likely resulted in the death of two or more of the hens.

This bunch of turkeys in all probability were with the gobbler that had just been killed an hour earlier. They wanted to get together but were very spooked and were taking no chances with their lives. They stayed in the thicket, moving very quickly through the small opening that we saw them pass through. When they did not see the hen that had been talking to them from my blind, they needed no further urging to depart the area. They would answer my calls but I could tell they were headed eastward to the river where life was not so hectic.

We just sat back in the blind and gave thanks to the powers that be for gracing our eyes once more with the beauty of day and for the thrill of the moment that we had just experienced. Another picture etched for all time in that album where we file all of the best ones. The storing process of the mind is strange. I find I can't remember what I did last week and yet I can recall in minute detail hunts that took place forty years ago.

I don't know if I am playing head games with myself in denying the fact that I am getting older or if it has just been a matter of priorities and I have placed the things I wanted on the tape for replay and let a great many others that I deemed unimportant go into the reject bin.

After a few more pulls on the wing bone, we stood up, stretched a bit, picked up our gear, and started our walk back to the Bronco, reading the multitude of signs in the sand road as we went along. Some of the tracks were superimposed over our own.

We rolled out of the hammock and went up to the house of Lyle Griffin. After a good hot cup of coffee, we were told by our genial host about the turn of events as they had transpired that morning relating to Mr. Quincy Adams. We in turn related our tale of woe. We thanked our host, reminding him that we had both reached the age that returning home with a light game bag bothered us not in the least. The exchange of calls that had eventually brought the flock within thirty-five steps of our blind was ample payment for our early rising.

After this opening day my companion and I hunted the following two mornings with no more success than that of the first day; even less if seeing a turkey was the measure of success.

The alarm clock jarred me out of a pleasant dream and I really wanted at that point to roll over and finish my dream. Just about the time I was starting to give credence to this thought the second alarm clock went off and this one will wake the dead. I stumbled over to the dresser and turned it off, flipped on the light, and looked at the face of the instrument of torture I held in my hands. It said 3:15.

Decisions are hard at 3:30 A.M. in the morning—coffee or hot tea, sausage and biscuit or biscuit, butter or fox grape jelly. Oh well, why not both with a cup of hot tea.

After this light repast, I relaxed in my recliner. I should have eaten at the table. I awoke with a start and all of the clocks in the house within my view read 4:10 A.M. Giving thanks that everything but the Ansley Fox had been packed the night before. I charged out, put the Fox in the gun rack and headed the short mile to the home of Mr. Van Dervort. On my arrival I saw not one light burning anywhere. This was most unusual because if this gentleman tells you he will be ready to go at 4:30, you may forget about the possibility of a delay. He will be ready, gun in hand. I sat in the vehicle for twenty minutes and then rang the door bell. He came to the door in pj's and a robe, and said that he had a very bad night and did not feel well enough to go. He told me to go without him.

I drove away feeling depressed but soon turned my thoughts to the outline of my hunt. I would be indeed alone on this day. Mr. Quincy had taken a sabbatical and I had the place I favored most on this property all to myself.

I set up my blind and then went about snipping a few small limbs that needed clearing out of my shooting lane. I collected a few palmetto fronds to stick in front of my blind. The gathering of all this was made swiftly and quickly with the use of a good set of pruning shears. I used a knife for years then found that pruning shears could do this job in a third of the amount of time it took with a knife. I place the small branches all about the blind netting then picked up a few strands of Spanish moss, hung them across the broom sage, worked them into the netting, and stepped back to view my handiwork. Daylight was just beginning to break. I looked at my setup once more then taking a hen decoy that I had brought along, I set it out in a position about thirty-five yards from my blind. The spot I had chosen to set the decoy could be seen by a gobbler that was looking for a hen but precluded my being shot by another hunter. I might also add that this blind was safe from a calling aspect. The blinds I build are always built with the safety factor foremost in mind.

I had an acquaintance that twice in one morning yelped up the same young man after changing his hunting area a half of a mile. The first time, he told the teenage lad that you can't creep up on a turkey but find a place turkeys are using, build a blind, sit still, and try to yelp one up. He then told him if you do creep up on a yelping turkey it is most likely to be a man in a blind. The lad shot him in the back with a .22 rifle that same afternoon and this man was in a wheelchair for several years until the medical profession evolved the technique to remove the bullet resting on his spinal cord. But the story is not ended. Three years later his wife was shot in the face while calling turkeys. The man that shot her was sure there was a turkey behind the bush he shot into because he could hear it yelping and saw it move. Turkey hunting is a safe sport if we make it so. The choice of a safe blind is always the first consideration. Make sure you have a large tree that covers your back, then be sure you can see clearly 180 degrees from left to right in front of your position. I have found if you scout an area well, you will find a number of places within the area that will provide you with a safe place to set up.

I have strayed a bit from our story of that morning on Turkey Island last spring but I am sure you will realize that we strayed in a sound direction.

I slipped through my opening and into my blind and sat down on my stool surveyed the area in front of me and was pleased. I flipped open the velcro locked pocket that held my favorite wing bone call secure. I pulled out the call, placed the bone between my lips, and cupped the bell of the trumpet between my hands to form a tone chamber. Leaving only a small opening below the little fingers to regulate the size of this hole. I can increase or decrease the volume of my calling. The turkey I was attempting to call was roosted almost 200 yards from my position, so the back side of my cupped hands were open quite wide. I clucked twice then twice more. I waited a few seconds and clucked twice again, following the clucks with six yelps rather fast and loud. I had an immediate answer in the form of a gobble, the first of eighty-two. It seemed that this fellow was about as talkative as one could hope for and I thought to myself that the game we were playing would be over with very soon. The-cards-all-falling-in-my-favor thought occurred during the first fifteen minutes of our contest, when this cheeky fellow would gobble five and six times. Each time he gobbled but would not move one step closer to the blind where I sat on the edge of my seat wondering what type of bird I was working with that would sometime gobble as much as eight times in answer to one or two yelps on the wing bone. The thought that this hunt might be over very quickly was soon dispelled.

It has been my experience that if I am working a bird that gobbles each time I call but will not move a peg in my direction I will do better to put my call aside for ten minutes or so before calling again. I find that in most cases the next time I call the turkey will have moved closer to my position, and sometime given ten or fifteen minutes it will be very close indeed. In some instances closer than you would have him. Like looking in the side of your blind. I had worked with this fellow for an hour and he had gobbled more than any turkey I had ever heard before. I recall on one occasion listened to a bird gobble fifty-two times at three o'clock one afternoon and had brought along Frank Schilling, the man who made the first turkey call I ever owned, which was a slate and a fat lighter wood peg inserted into a corn cob. The next morning at daybreak, I was using the same piece of slate that he had given me ten years before, but now it had a cedar peg driven into a cedar block.

We walked to the bank of the Withlocoochee River and looked north. I yelped and clucked, waited a minute or so, and did it again. At this last series of yelps, the fellow that had gobbled fifty-two times the afternoon before was 500 yards west of us. He pitched off of a limb and flew across the river to our side. We swiftly built a palmetto frond blind of sorts. I yelped once more and he ran to us, gobbling intermittently between steps. He stopped, gobbled, and ran to the small flat where we sat waiting.

He stopped thirty yards away from our blind behind a large strip of palmettos and there we could hear but not see him strutting, puffing, rattling his tail feathers, and dragging his wing tips. I clucked one time and purred. Suddenly he rounded the palmetto clump and jumped up onto a fallen pine log. I nodded my head to my companion and he turned the humpback Browning twelve-gauge auto loose. The young gobbler began to fan the earth on his last flight to the roost where he would secure for all time to come.

We looked at the bird, a fine, fat, two-year-old. At three o'clock the afternoon before I was unable to move him an inch and yet he would respond to each call I made with a gobble or many gobbles. Now as I recall this hunt he only gobbled six times after flying across the river and none while he was roosted on the other side. I think less than twelve minutes elapsed from the time he flew across the river until he jumped on the fallen pine log. They come easy at times, but not often.

The bird that gobbled eighty-two times in a little over a hour had stopped and this bird if he moved at all from the sound of his gobbling seemed to be moving east toward the river and away from me. I would cluck and cut then yelp, and I could tell from his response that he had marched back to a spot very close to where he flew down then he would gobble. I put my wing bone back into my vest pocket and just sat back looking out of the blind. I pushed the catch lever and broke open the barrels on the Fox. I lifted out the duplex loads of 4 × 6 in the left hand barrel and 4 × 6 in the right and then slipped them back in and rebreeched the gun. Time, it seems, is never just as we would have it, if we want it to race, it stands still. If we would have it stand still, it seems to race.

I looked at my watch for what was probably the tenth time in as many minutes as I said to myself, "I will wait five more minutes more before I call again." About this time I heard two or three hens very close to me, giving forth with low yelping, clucks, purring, and other conversational small talk.

I broke my resolve and pulled out my slate and peg, as the birds were within thirty steps. I clucked, low purred, and yelped three times very softly. The hens called back but held their ground.

I let five minutes go by and went through the same sequence of calls and almost before I could stop yelping there was an earth shaking gobble—just one, but it was within twenty steps of my blind. I eased the slate and peg to the ground beneath my stool and tightened my grip on the Fox, slipping the piece from safe to fire at the same time, although I could not see into the area where the sound of the gobble was made due to the thickness of the foliage. I began to train my eyes on the first semiopen area on my lefthand side. I waited, my mouth getting drier by the second. I eased a look at my watch; five minutes had passed and no sound was audible other than crows calling in the swamp, deviling an owl. I eased my hand down and picked up my slate and peg. I clucked once and put it down. At that instant a gobbler ran at half speed into the area I had been watching.

He was not taking any chances with his life. He ran through low bush foliage with only his head and neck exposed. He never slowed down but it was apparent that he was looking for the hen that had been talking to him for so long. As he ran he was looking sideways at the flat that I had the hen decoy set up on, but if he ever saw her he gave no indication of it for as the saying goes, he never slowed down for coal or water but just kept rolling. The gobbler had been in my view for perhaps fifteen yards when he passed the opening I wanted him to reach. I touched off the lethal load of copper-plated four-by-six's and stood up. I unbreeched my gun and seeing that there was no need to reload, I removed the other shell and walked the thirty-nine yards to where my gobbler had just fluttered his last.

He was a fine young gobbler, weighing seventeen and a half pounds with a five-inch beard. A two-year-old that was as cautious as most four-year-olds. I put my turkey strap on his head and neck and headed for the truck. I was very happy with my sixty-five-year-old shotgun.

I stopped to rest at a place we call the old hog pen. I sat there for a few minutes and looked around me drinking in all of the sounds and the beauty around me. Counting myself fortunate to be alive and wondering how many times I would be privileged to walk this sand trail that goes by the hog pen and be awed by the incomparable beauty of this place.

Calls and Calling

I honestly believe that most serious turkey hunters can remember the first call that they bought, made or had been given to them. It may be improper to equate this with our first love affair but I really don't think I am too far off base in making that comparison. I can hear my daughter saying, "Insensitive chauvinist talk." Well, perhaps. In any case I remember well my first turkey call. It was a piece of roofing slate that was four and one-half inches long by three inches wide by one-eighth of an inch thick. It came with a corn cob that had a fat lighter (rosin-filled pine splinter) peg stuck in it. The call was a good one. The peg was rounded on the end and was about one-half inch wide. It was given to me in 1953 by Frank Schilling, a friend who was almost like a second father.

To say that this call has served me well would be a gross understatement, for this slate has been the mainstay used in the harvesting of well over eighty-five turkeys in my lifetime, and although I now have many other types of calls, I still favor the slate and peg. I changed the corn cob and lighter peg to one of cedar along with the peg and the block that forms the tone. In my twenty-eight-year tenure with the Florida Game and Fresh Water Fish Commission, I was privileged to have access to some of the finest turkey woods throughout the state. Over the years, I have called literally hundreds of birds within shooting range for my own entertainment and that of others, while at the same time, I was also perfecting my calling. I still derive a great deal of satisfaction from doing this. I would not have you believe that every turkey that answers my call comes to the blind, but I will say that if I have time to work the bird, I can normally bring it in about seventy percent of the time. We are speaking now of fall turkeys that are scattered and of gobblers in the spring season. I have had a measure of success over the years by walking through the woods, yelping at intervals in an effort to pick up an answer, but I will state that for the most part this has been slow going. If I had to draw a graph depicting the success ratio of this method on a scale from one to ten, I would mark it at about four. I will say that in gobbling season, walking from one place to another and calling every 200 yards or so will sometimes bring about the placing of your turkey strap around the head and feet of the Thanksgiving Day bird, but for me it has never worked well.

In the last thirty years I have used a wing bone for this type of calling. It is easy to use and when used well it really sounds like a turkey. I carry mine on a braided nylon lanyard around my neck to prevent loss. My wing bone trumpet call also fits into a pocket of my turkey hunting vest as well, when I am not using it. Sherry Van Dervort, wife of my hunting companion, made a vest for me that holds five shells, my wing bone trumpet call, diaphragm calls, bug dope, slate call and pegs, surveyor tape, cough drops, etc. All pockets are sealed by Velcro so nothing can be lost in transit from the truck to the blind in the hours of darkness before the owl begins to hoot. Shortly after she made this vest for me, Mrs. Van Dervort asked me how I liked the product of her expertise.

As I recall, I believe I told her that I would fight the entire Cuban army over it.

In an age where much of what we purchase gives us so little true pleasure and trouble free use, this vest is a wellspring of joy and to make it better, it was a gift. I never have to fumble or search for anything, even in pitch black darkness, for each thing I use is in its own pocket, always. I will say to anyone who is interested in having a vest of this type made that your wife, girlfriend, or mother more than likely knows a good seamstress in your neighborhood that will make you a vest of this type for less than thirty dollars. Show the seamstress the size and shape of the things you want to carry and remind her that you want all pockets to have Velcro all the way across not just Velcro tabs. It is bad to have a pocket open up and drop your favorite slate and peg somewhere along the walk from the boat or truck to your blind and never recover it. I have five shell loops of black elastic that fit each shell tightly. Each person's wants may differ, but you will wonder how you ever got along without your own vest once you have one.

Turkey calls of all types are dear to the hearts of any serious hunter of this bird. I carry with me, each time I go into the woods, a number of calls of different types and I find I am no different than most of my friends and other serious hunters that I know. In forty-five years of buying, testing, making, and manufacturing turkey calls for sale, I do believe I have used about every type of call ever devised to lure a wild turkey. About the time I became thirty years old, I even had a dentist friend make me an upper plate call. This was before the mouth yelper had reached the market. The upper plate call had a U-shaped pair of gold arms that held a strip of rubber daming and when used properly, it sounded much the same as the mouth diaphragm of today. A short time after the dentist gave me the upper plate call, I found my first mouth yelper for sale in a sporting goods store. It was made by Penn's Woods Calls. If I remember correctly, I gave two dollars and fifty cents for this call. It was a good one. Within a month of hard practice I had arrived at a point that I could give good yelps, clucks, and kee-kee runs, and other than cutting and cackling I have added very little to my repertoire with this type of yelper since that day. I find that in the fall of the year, when one has a flock of this year's turkeys well scattered, there is hardly a better call to use after a wait of twenty to thirty minutes than the kee-kee run combined with two or three yelps at the end of the run. Nothing can give this better than a good mouth call.

I like the mouth yelper and for the past twenty-five years with this call I have enticed a lot of turkeys to come take a little closer look at the area twenty yards in front of my blind. The mouth yelper has a lot going for it. You can have both hands on your gun and can be looking at the bird standing just out of shotgun range, stretching his neck, looking for you and needing just one more cluck or one more low yelp, just one, to convince it that another turkey is just ahead. If you are good, you can give that one call that starts him on his way to you once more, closing the distance to that point of no return, and you will not have to move anything but your gun at the moment of truth. The really good mouth yelper must sound just like another turkey to a turkey and then they are deadly.

Last season I almost lost a big gobbler that I had been talking to with a wing bone trumpet call. I had left my blind to ease up to a point fifty yards closer to a spot where the foliage opened up a wee bit, making a basketball size hole that I could look through as well as shoot through. When I reached this opening I felt for my wing bone and then discovered to my dismay that I had left it hanging on a limb back at my blind. I reached into my shirt pocket and came up with a pill box and in it I found a three-reed mouth call given to me by my friend Lamar Williams of Stark, Florida, the manufacturer of a fine line of turkey calls. I flipped this call into my mouth and yelped three times. The turkey ran out of the deep woods and stood facing me at ninety yards where he strutted then gobbled. This action took place for the better part of ten minutes, but I could not bring him an inch in my direction. He had gobbled fifteen times while standing there. I could see by his last few movements that he might be getting ready to leave the open flat he was gobbling on and return to the hammock, as he could not see the hen that had just been yelping to him. I clucked once and he gobbled.

At this point I rested the back of my left hand on top of a fence post that was placed there by a farmer in years past (I think by divine providence). I put the forearm of my little 218 M. Bee Martini in the palm of my left hand on top of the post, looked through the four-power scope, the cross hairs settled at the apex of this gobbler's pulley bone and started a slow squeeze on the trigger. The report shattered the early morning air like a jet breaking the sound barrier. The bird flew into the air six feet high and then flew back north of where he had been standing. When he had covered fifty yards in flight, he hit the ground and started walking to the east. He walked very fast, tail straight back and head low and forward. He did this for perhaps eighty yards. I started cutting excitedly and yelping fast, and then he did the unbelievable.

Within two minutes of being shot at he almost came to a skidding halt, turned and faced my position, fluffed up, and began to gobble to my cutting and fast yelps.

He was now about 140 yards north of me and eighty yards east. He put on quite a show for perhaps five minutes. I still tried to sound excited in my yelping, but I had toned it down a bit. I gave one more set of excited cuts and yelps and with this he rose and flew across a small pond and landed behind three oak trees growing in a cluster forty yards east of my position. I could see only his head now and then in the forks of the oaks. He would gobble and his head would disappear, then he would strut and drum. I looked through the scope once more and said to myself, "When he comes around the oak tree on the south I will take him."

I got set and clucked twice, then yelped low three times. This is the beauty of the diaphragm, I had never moved my head nor my hands. The only movement I made at this time was the gradual tightening of my finger on the trigger as the gobbler stepped from behind the southernmost oak in full strut. He was a fine nineteen-and-a-half-pound bird with a ten-and-a-half-inch beard and spurs one and a half inches long.

I could go on continuously relating success stories much the same as the one just told, all of them brought to the desired ending by the use of a mouth call. Yet, as good as it is and as successful as I have been in using it. It is not my favorite call. However, for giving certain calls, nothing can beat it. I would feel a bit uncomfortable if I wanted to give a kee-kee run followed by a yelp or two and couldn't find a diaphragm call in my hunting bag. I would hate to be in the woods without one.

The history of the turkey wing bone call and its use in luring the wild turkey has been lost in antiquity. I am sure the use of this call as a hunting device took place somewhere along the path of time mankind has traveled to a point somewhere between the time we stopped wearing skins with the hair on them and the time that someone dreamed up the use of a loom to weave cloth. Perhaps one of our relatives from the distant past was sitting around the lodge fire and in nibbling a bit of this and that decided to crack both ends of a wing bone to suck out the marrow and in doing so said, "Say, when you suck this just right it sounds almost like a hen turkey!" The thoughts just penned might or might not have been the way this revelation came about, but in any event we who turkey hunt and use this device owe the fellow who made this wonderful discovery a large debt of gratitude, because in doing so this fellow opened the door to the use of one of the deadliest turkey calls ever devised by man. In its simplest form it is the smallest of the two bones from the second section of a hen turkey's wing. It is boiled, cleaned by light scraping and both ends are cut off with a very small file one and a half inches from the end of the bone. A small auto spark plug file works well for this job. A pipe cleaner is then pulled through to clean the inside of marrow. This section of bone just as it is, in the hands of a man who can use it, will toll many birds along their last path to his blind.

Many old time Florida turkey hunters always carried two or three bones in a pocket somewhere about their person and if asked could always produce a coon bone toothpick, a wing bone, and a good brand of pocket knife. Times have changed a lot since the period I speak of. If we were to ask 100 men on the street today to reveal the contents of their pockets, we might find ten who were carrying a good knife—and this in a rural area—but we would find no coon bone toothpicks or turkey wing bones. The wing bone can be used in this short form, but I have found that the addition of a trumpet barrel, much the same as used on a good duck call, gives more volume and better control of the notes. The extension of a six- to seven-inch barrel also makes this call much easier to hold with both hands at the bottom end of the trumpet and by opening one hand more volume can be obtained and by closing the hand the calling becomes more muted.

A lot of wing bone calls are made by the use of three bones taken from a hen turkey's body, dried, then glued together with epoxy. I have a call that I think highly of that was given to me by Lovett Williams, maker of a set of cassettes, *Real Turkeys*, this set of tapes has real birds gobbling, yelping, purring, clucking, and many other calls. A wonderful aid to anyone that is trying to learn to call. This one is made with the use of two bones and it is a good one. I also have another call made by call maker Lamar Williams that utilizes two bones. This call gives a rather coarse, deep, throaty yelp. I find this call to be the easiest wing bone to control that I have ever used and when using it I rarely make a mistake.

The late V. O. Johnson of Gould Ark made a very fine wing bone type of trumpet call. He also made recorded instructions to teach you to call. In corresponding with Mrs. Johnson, I was informed of her husband's death and that a tornadotype storm had rolled through that section of town and the factory was partly destroyed in a storm, but will reopen soon. The whole call was turned on a small wood lathe, and each one was very fancy and was made of one solid piece of wood. The mouthpiece of this call is wood as the whole call is turned as one piece. The calls given on this trumpet are very good indeed. I had to replace the mouthpiece on the one I have due to a mishap that damaged it. I did so by putting the top portion of 30-06 cartridge over the end of the call after it had been worked down to fit. Then taking a wing bone that had been wrapped with silk thread till it would almost fit snugly inside the 06 brass, I filled it with a good grade of epoxy. With this call I have killed a large number of turkeys. I find that it leaves little to be desired. One of the great advantages of the wing bone is that it can be used in rainy weather; in fact it can become completely wet with no fear of false calls or tone changes.

I recall two occasions that lend credence to the above statement. I was on a spring gobbler hunt in the Lochloosa management area at Cross Creek, Florida, and the weather had been on the blustery side since daybreak with light showers coming and going all morning. I had started to walk along a two-rutted trail with palmettos waist high on each side and stands of pine trees twenty years and older running along both sides as far as the eye could see.

I was moving much faster than I wanted to but the sky east of me was becoming darker by the minute and I could hear the ominous rumble of heavy thunder as I headed west to a large flat that held a great deal of turkey sign and activity. At the moment though, if I am to be truthful, I was thinking less of hunting and more of a rather large cattle feeder that had a good, sound tin roof, which stood on the southeast edge of the pine flat that I was hoping to reach before the rain came in full force. In looking back at the sky east of me, I could tell that when the clouds reached the spot I was headed to the bottom was going to fall out and when it did it would be a toad strangler. I was right in my assessment of the weather and the amount of rain that fell. I had almost 100 yards to go to reach the shelter of the cattle feeder when I was caught by the full force of it. In seconds most all that I had on was completely wet, as were most of the contents of my pockets. I kept up a slow march in the direction of the feeder box, the rain falling now in sheets and so hard I was unable to see forty feet ahead. In time I reached the cattle feeder and slipped in under the roof.

After about thirty minutes or so the storm abated and only a light sprinkle of rain was falling. I moved out of the shelter and almost as soon as I stepped out I thought I heard a turkey yelp to the east of me. Then it yelped once more, and on hearing this I placed my wing bone between my lips and gave a medium loud cluck followed by some very loud and long lost calling. I received an answer that came while I was still yelping. It was very loud and snappy. I stood with my back to a huge longleaf pine and as I stood there a light rain began to fall again. I was glad I had the wing bone. I cut loose with another series of lost calls and cutting. Three turkeys rose from the palmettos and flew through the rain into the pine trees around me from a distance of about one hundred and fifty yards. I looked through my binoculars at all three very closely and determined that they were all hens. I did attempt to call the hens closer to my tree just to boost my dripping ego, but I could see very soon that once settled in their respective trees, they were not going to move as they had settled in for a while. They yelped a time or two then called the whole thing off. Squatting low on the limb they took their ease and for all I know may have remained on the limb til the next morning as they are sometimes prone to do in really wet and bad weather. I left the flat in midafternoon, and they were still there when I peeked through my glass.

I can think of only two calls that would work well under the conditions just described. One is the roof of the mouth yelper and the other is the turkey wing bone. Like a first class duck or goose call, water and rain mean nothing when it comes to their performance. I recall the opening day of the gobbling season in 1988. It rained hard in intermittent squalls from long before daylight till 9:30 A.M., with the wind rising in gusts as high as twenty-five to thirty miles per hour from time to time. At 9:30 the rain stopped and the wind dropped in intensity to gusts of five to 15 miles per hour. I had placed a turkey decoy northeast of my blind about thirty-three yards away and was sitting in a palmetto thicket with a military camo net in front of me as a blind and a big live oak to my back. I was wet and so was almost everything I had with me but the weather was clearing and only the wind made for hard hunting. I reached into my jacket pocket and brought out my wing bone.

As I have stated before, this type of turkey call is no fair weather friend. You will find it ready to do business when you are, wet or dry. It yelps, clucks, cackles, kee-kee runs, soft, low, medium or loud. Whatever you want you can get once you master it. The beauty of the call is that it sounds so much like a turkey when the person using it can really call with it. Once you have paid your dues and get your calling right with the wing bone trumpet call, you will pull more birds—the ones with the long beards—than you ever thought possible.

Let us return to that very wet opening day of four seasons ago. I had been giving two or three medium loud clucks followed by five or six loud yelps at five-minute intervals, then straining to hear, above the wind, a sound that would give me some assurance that there was still a gobbler or two that hadn't drowned in the morning deluge. A short time after 10 A.M. something told me to look away from my decoy. I slowly looked back to my right and there, standing in a gallberry tunnel at the base of a huge live oak, was one of the largest gobblers anyone could ever hope to see. He was fluffed out in full strut, looking at the hen decoy. His wattles were bright red in excitement, and he had a beard that seemed to almost touch the ground at his feet. How long he had been looking at her I will never know, however, I do know my look at him was of short duration for almost before I could turn slightly to my right and raise my gun he had stepped behind the huge live oak.

I placed the fluorescent bead front sight of my gun at a spot I thought the gobbler's head would be when he reached the north side of the oak and said to myself, "When he comes around the tree headed for the decoy I will roll him." This fellow had made up his mind that my hen decoy was a little bit too haughty in her demeanor or did not move enough to please him so he walked off through the cypress swamp in six inches of water to the dry ground on the far east side of the swamp, gobbled one time to tell her where he had gone, and called it a day. As far as his departure was concerned I don't believe that this old boy saw me. I feel he was just nervous and not taking chances with his life. I stayed till 12:30 P.M. changing blinds from time to time, clucking, purring, and yelping all to no avail. However, I am sure this old fellow and I did meet once more four days later near the same spot where he gave that one gobble, but I will tell you that story in another chapter titled "The Wonderful Remington 870."

I have owned and made box calls with the hinged lids, the type referred to as the gipson call in the grand old book *The American Wild Turkey* written by Henry E. Davis. It was long out of print, but now available from Lovette Williams, Cedar Key, Florida. I have owned two very good gipson-type calls. One was a lynch call, one of the first made in the late fifties. The other was made of pure red cedar, both box and lid, by an old man who lived in Otter Creek, Florida, about 1955. His name is lost to me as is the fine call he made. I have only the memory of his fine cabinet making and the splendid tone of the yelps and clucks this call produced.

I have never been a great fan of this type of call for a number of reasons, therefore at the time I wrote this I had never killed a turkey using this type of call. I dislike the size of the good ones and you must keep something between the lid and the sides of the box or it will yelp on its own as you walk along. I did, however, hear a fellow using a primos box call with a hinged lid a short time ago and it made me think that an old dog might be taught new tricks. I seek to be, after all, a perfectionist in my hunting and if I think one call has an edge on another, you can bet on the fact that I am on the way to the store to buy one of them. The primos box the fellow was using gave perfect clucks, yelps, cackles, whines, and gobbles that made my hair stand on end. A fellow would have to choose his blind well when using this call and be careful in every respect to prevent an accidental shooting because the gobble made with this call sounds as good as that of gobbler himself.

The young turkey hunter of today has a vast array of calls to choose from, in fact so many that the choice might become confusing were it not for the fact that most of them are surprisingly good. It has not always been quite this easy to obtain a really good call. When I began to hunt most good turkey calls were made and kept by the maker or given to the young sons of your hunting companions when you were sure that they had reached a point that they really wanted to learn to call turkeys and you were ready to teach them. The state of Florida has been fortunate in being one of the few states that have a good, huntable population of turkeys and that until recent years suffered no great loss of habitat. In some sections of the state that contained good habitat, turkeys were hunted to the point of being extinct, and were brought back due to the restocking program and studies done by Lovett Williams and David Austin. Perhaps these factors have always kept the interest in turkey hunting high in the state and because of this a person has not had to look too hard to find a turkey call of some type from many sources within the state. In years past I have brought excellent wing bone and box calls in small hardware stores and country filling stations from the south side of Lake Okeechobee to Panama City. It always took time to sort through the box of calls til I found the one that suited me, but in those days things moved slow and this was okay with the shop owner.

Not too far from Lake Okeechobee, there is a fellow by the name of Tom Gaskins, who lives just a few miles off the west shore of the lake in the small town of Palmdale. This fellow makes one of the best box calls I have ever used or seen. It is unbelievable just how easy this call is to use and how good the tone of this little yelper really is. I have one that was given to me by my old compadre Frank Schilling in 1953. I was going through a series of clucks, yelps, purring, and putting with this call a few nights ago and I am amazed at how much this little box sounds like a turkey when played back on the tape recorder. It is a deadly call in the woods also. Tom told me that he rarely ever did anything but cluck in using this call as he found that was all he ever really needed. However, I will say that I have owned three of his calls and have two now and I know that each call I have owned has been capable of a full range of turkey talk of the finest kind. If the reader ever, perchance, gets to Palmdale, Florida, Mr. Gaskins has a cypress knee museum that will keep him spellbound for an hour or two, and who knows you might even get to see your turkey call made while you watch.

Down that way, but at the Gulf Coast town of Fort Myers, there was a man by the name of Jim Potteroff who made a small box call and it went by the name of "the Jim Potteroff world championship turkey call." It was a fine little call. I haven't seen one of these calls in any of the stores around the state in a number of years now, but perhaps it is still being made and sold locally. Box calls of this type need a bit of chalk and a small piece of slate or a cedar striker three inches long by three-quarters of an inch square. The lip of the box extends about a half inch beyond the tone chamber on most calls of this type and this lip must be chalked as does as the striker before each series of calls. The striker is drawn across the lip much the same as a bow is drawn across the strings of a violin to produce the sound wanted. The good ones are very good indeed and I have yelped up many turkeys playing around with this type of call. I have also killed some very big gobblers using the small box calls.

I have had a number of people, over the years, ask me if I could have the use of only three types of calls what would they be, and then if I could only have the use of two, and then of course the use of only one call. This sounds like a difficult choice to make, but it really isn't. If by decree, I could only have three calls, they would be, the diaphragm, the wing bone, and the slate and peg. If restricted to two calls it would be the wing bone trumpet call and the slate and peg. If I could have the use of only one call and that alone, it would be the slate and peg.

Often I am asked why the slate is my choice and my answer is three fold.

1. Versatility—you can do so much with a slate and peg, it will give perfect clucks, yelps, cuts, purrs, and putts, and give each call high or low in the exact range of sound you want projected to the turkey.
2. Reliability—once you have really mastered it, the slate will give you everything you need to call a turkey, whether you are working a bird at a distance or have him within thirty steps of your blind.

Once you have gained complete control and have paid your dues with the hours it takes to get there you will become as consistent as a metronome, being able to give one or a hundred perfect yelps, clucks, purrs, cuts and whines at will and you will never make a mistake, or not any a turkey can discern.

3. And last, but never let this be forgotten, a good slate with a peg match to the slate (and you may have to try five or six different pegs to get one with the proper tone) used correctly will fool more turkeys than any other type of call and it will fool them when they are standing fifteen feet away from your blind.

I have had turkeys walk up and stick their head into my blind after I had clucked low and purred on my old slate. I have come to believe that when I do my part right the slate and peg I have used for the past thirty-six years will sound as much like a turkey to a turkey, as another turkey.

If a turkey cannot be called up—and some cannot be—the slate will bring it in. When other calls fail it will work and it will work even on birds that are call shy, three weeks into the gobbling season.

Most of us have hunted on property where the birds have been called up and frightened several times before the season opens. By the time the legal gobbling season is in full swing a lot of the long beards will answer your calls, but will head in a direction away from your position. The older birds now expect you to come to them and join the rest of the hens in their party. This bird can be exasperating but given time, a little later in the morning when all of his hens have left him and gone to their nest, this sly fellow can still be called up and brought home. The style of calling must be changed just as the actions of the gobbler have changed. The thing to remember is that turkeys that are really scared are not very vocal and almost any calling they do will be low and muted. A lot of answering calls you receive will be clucks. The calls you use on this bird under the conditions just described must be soft. The calls you will give should be soft clucks and purrs for the most part, a few low—and I repeat low—yelps of no more than three or four notes. As to the interval of timing between your call, I believe thirty minutes is not too long to wait. Always keep it uppermost in your mind that you are working with birds that are frightened. Some of them have been called up close enough to identify the caller as a man and on public hunt areas this may have occurred a number of times.

Many turkeys today now gobble once or twice and that is it for the day, but if your calling is soft and good enough and you can stay in your blind till noon, you may have one or two late morning gobblers check the area around your blind. You may hear a cluck or two but most of the time. At this stage of the game, your contact with this bird will be visual. You will look down at your feet inside your blind and when you look up, he will be standing there. When this occurs it is good to have your gun resting across your lap. This is where a good blind is a real comfort because you are able to lean your gun against a tree, fight flying insects, take a sip of coffee, use slate and box calls, and any number of things that require movement of your hands and body with the sure knowledge that done slowly, none of this will be seen by the turkey.

In our discussion of calls and calling, we have yet to touch on the most perfect instrument that can be used to call turkeys, that of the human voice. I am sure the reason for this is that so few people can do it effectively. In my lifetime I have met only two people who can do this and do it well. I have heard others try and although they may hit a note right now and then and might even be able to call up a bird on occasion, this is not what we are speaking of. We are speaking of using the mouth and throat as an instrument to give a full range of perfect calls that can be given when needed in a specific situation while hunting turkeys. As I said before, in all of my turkey hunting experience, I have only met two people whom I consider good at this. At the time I met them both men were in the employment of the Game Management Division of the Florida Game and Fresh Water Fish Commission and both were assigned to the commission's turkey study and restoration program at Fish Eating Creek and the area around Avon Park, Florida.

The two men I speak of are Lovett Williams and Robert Phillips. Personally I know only a handful of men who have devoted the time and effort to study the wild turkey to the extent that this pair of fellows have. Both are woodsmen and hunters without peer and both men have devoted a lifetime of study in the field, and in Lovett's case, in the classroom as well. Both have given full measure to the preservation of this bird we all love so well, each striving to increase its habitat where possible and trying to hang on to the existing habitat we still have. I wish it were possible that everyone who knows what good turkey calling is could hear the calls both of these fellow give: a series of different calls using nothing but their vocal cords.

I also wish that everyone who loves the wild turkey could sit down and talk with both men for an hour or so. I do not recall Lovett ever telling me that he used this rare talent in hunting turkeys, however, I do know that he is, like myself, a lover of the wing bone. He may just keep this vocal talent handy to put fellows like me in awe of another one of his many abilities. In any event if he used it consistently in his hunting it could be as deadly as the fowl pox.

The other man I write of, Bob Phillips, is able to give a full range of calls with his mouth and vocal cords, and the calls given are very good indeed. He has a good ear for pitch, tone, and timing. He also plays string instruments of several types and after taking a dram or two of Baker County cough medicine to help alleviate the dryness of his throat, which I assume might be caused by the strain on his vocal cords due to yelping, he can do a fine job of singing. He is a good turkey hunter himself and has passed this part of his woodsmanship down the line to his children; the oldest son having honed his turkey hunting skills to the degree that he now does a good bit of guiding and yelping up birds for others. I have sat on the judge's bench with Mr. Phillips, acting as judge also in a number of calling contest over the years. I have found that at the end of each contest when we compare our rating sheets that we are only a point or two off in our scoring of each contestant, so we must hear tones and timing in about the same range.

Before leaving this chapter on calls and calling, I must mention Lamar Williams, the turkey call manufacturer from Stark, Florida. Mr. Williams makes a fine line of calls. This line encompasses a full range of turkey calls, slates and wooden pegs, even slates mounted in box turtle shells, slates and acrylic pegs, corncob pegs box calls, box and lid calls, wing bone calls, and mouth yelpers. All of the calls made in Mr. Williams' shop are hand tuned and they are fine. In addition to this he is a fellow who is a woodsman and a turkey hunter second to none and knows what a good call should sound like. I will also state that this man is beyond a doubt, the best all around turkey caller that I have ever had the pleasure of listening to. He can yelp, cluck, putt, purr, cackle, and kee-kee gobble. You name the calls and he can deliver them on demand and on any type of device ever made to call up a turkey.

He is also one of the finest men that I have ever known when it comes to sharing his many skills and giving advice to anyone getting started in turkey hunting. He is never condescending when asked a question, but always kind, polite, and helpful. This is another man I have been privileged to sit on the judge's bench with in a number of calling contests. I have also conducted a number of hunting seminars with this gentleman and have always come away awed by his calling ability. As of late, time has a way of slipping past me and I lose track of it but I do believe that seven years ago or thereabouts Lamar gave me a wing bone call that beats any call of this type that I have even used thus far, and I have used a great many. I have others that are good and some have wonderful tones, but this one has it all plus an additional quality. With this one, it is a rare occasion that I ever make a mistake or false call. I feel that when you find a call like that it should be listed as a national treasure.

As a closing statement about this man I would like to state that his son almost always attended the turkey seminars with his father and was a big help to him in carrying and setting up his display. It was always pleasing to me to note that this lad always said, "Yes, sir," "No, sir," and "Thank you," when these responses were appropriate. To me, this was as refreshing as a rain shower on a hot and humid day. We have lost so many of the amenities since the 1960s, and I often wonder why. How did it all come about and in such a short period of time?

Somewhere about the middle of 1989 I was browsing through a videotape section at Dan's Gun Room in Inverness, Florida, and I picked up a tape titled *Spring Fever.* I read the back portion of the tape that told of the contents of the film and in doing so I decided to take it home for a day or two and watch it. I am glad I did. If you really enjoy turkey hunting you are in for a thrill. If you are a beginning turkey hunter or even if you have hunted for years, you will enjoy this tape. You will be amazed by the outstanding calling and bird working done by Danny Kretzer. On this videotape you will hear some of the finest turkey calling and you will see some of the best bird working ever done by anyone on film. He seems to have the gobblers that he works on this tape tied to a snap swivel on a leash because once they begin to work to his calling there is just no turning back.

There is one sequence on this tape in which Mr. Kretzer is using a corncob head with hard wood peg insert on round glass call. He is calling to a fine gobbler and the calls being given are a very rapid series of loud cuts, clucks, and yelps. This segment of the film displays, for me at least, the epitome of the excitement of turkey hunting. In viewing this few minutes of the tape, I find all of the elements of the hunt that brings each one of us back day after day, season after season. We may be tired, worn out, two days short on sleep, but who cares, we are still there. Age matters not a fig. The alarm clock rings at 3:30 A.M. and we get up. I am sixty-five years of age as I sit writing this, one of my constant turkey hunting companions is fifty-nine and the other, Mr. John Q. Adams, is seventy-six years of age, and John Q is always at the swamp's edge ready to go.

Mr. Kretzer in his calling on *Spring Fever* exhibits complete control and well he should. He was twice the winner of the Maryland state turkey championship calling contest. After viewing the film, I knew I had to have a call like the one he used in the making of this film. I was pleased to find out through our correspondence that he manufactured the call and several mouth calls as well. Mr. Kretzer's company goes by the name of Oak Ridge Turkey Calls, and I should add that I have two of the glass and corncob striker calls, plus several of his mouth yelpers. All are very good, although I must admit I cannot, as yet, coax the sound from the glass and corncob call in the manner that Danny Kretzer does, but then I have not been the Maryland state calling champion twice in a lifetime.

But let us return to the calls. Most of us have two or three types of calls that we carry, and those of us who have been chasing this bird for forty years may have a cabinet full. While some of us take every possible precaution to keep each call functional and in good condition with special care given to the calls we have carried for forty years, many do not. I know a fellow who throws all of his calls in a bag and piles his gun in on top of them. My best slate is wrapped in tanned deer hide and carried in a Prince Albert tobacco can painted black. The cedar peg that is used with this slate is carried in a Ziplock sandwich bag because unvarnished cedar will soak up any type of fluid. I take great care to keep bug dope, gun oil, water, boot cream, and anything else that I feel might cause the tone to change in this perfect turkey calling instrument away from it.

If anyone believes that an excellent call cannot be destroyed by soaking in any of the liquids I have listed, please let me refer back to the fine lynch call I purchased in the late fifties.

I could make excellent yelps—both hen and gobbler, clucks, cuts, purrs, and gobble. This call I hand-picked out of about two dozen in a sporting goods store in Tallahassee. Believe me, this box left very little to be desired in the way of a turkey calling instrument. I had never heard a better hinged-lid box call when I purchased this one. At the time I bought this call, I had a friend who was a real power in turkey hunting, a master of the wing bone. I made the mistake of letting him hear this Lynch box. I took it through its bag of tricks and before I had finished my last call, he was trying to arrive at some sort of bargain to get it. I knew how badly he wanted this call and I said to myself that I would pick up another like it when I flew back into Tallahassee in the next week or so. As it so often is in life, it was about five years before I found another Lynch call that pleased me almost as well as that one, and I got talked out of this one too. It ended up as the first turkey call of a thirteen-year-old lad by the name of Corvel Justisin in Deer Park, Florida. The call I gave the old-time wing bone hunter served him well for almost a year and then one day he put it in a box along with some gun oil. The oil can lid let go one day and soaked the box, the rag that had been wrapped around the call, and all else that was there. The next time I saw and tried to use that fine yelper, it was so oil soaked, it would not make a sound. I advised him to obtain some commercial solvent and to soak the call each day with this and then rub all of the oil away as it surfaced and repeat again each day for a week or so. I never saw this call again, so he must have failed and was too embarrassed to tell me.

I have found Rubbermaid® sandwich boxes to be very good to keep slate and peg calls in, and they also work well for keeping mouth yelpers clean and handy. The kitchenware department of Walmart stores and the same department in Walgreens drug stores have several sizes of plastic containers that will house most of your calls, keeping them clean and safe.

In closing let me say that when you find a yelper that you are able to use to perfection, one that calls turkeys up to the ten-yard point in front of your blind; one that can give twenty yelps in a lost call and never break in tone, volume, or cadence; one that can deliver a soft putt, a medium cluck, or the loudest yelp ever wanted each time you call on it; in short, a call that you can depend on under all conditions—when you find a call like this, if you are wise you will:

1. Never loan it to anyone.
2. Keep it under lock and key.
3. Be careful of oils and even insect repellent on wooden portions. Be particularly careful with cedar for it will soak up repellent each time you use your call unless you wipe the inside of your hands.

4. Never leave it on the dash of your vehicle. The heat inside a locked car can reach 180 degrees and this can cause a rapid tone change in some calls and some woods become dry and split. Some glue will soften and let go.
5. Use some type of hard cover to keep it in.
6. If chalk must be used on your caller use the very cheapest dime store children's blackboard chalk. High-grade wax chalk used in schools is not good as the wax coating on it tends to cause most calls to screech and false call. White carpenters chalk is good also.

I will close this with one last statement: Before many who are now reading this book were born, there was an older lady by the name of Sophie Tucker who sang in night-clubs and on the stage, before the advent of television. At any of her engagements, one song was always requested before the night was over, and it always brought down the house. The song was "A Good Man Is Hard To Find." The same can be said of turkey calls.

Reflections

In looking back on my hunting career, I know that I was very fortunate to have the instructions that I received from relatives and friends when I reached the point where I really became serious about my turkey hunting. It seems that when I had a problem there was always someone at my side helping me solve it. I know that learning the daily habits of the eastern and the Osceola wild turkey and applying what I had learned to my hunting techniques on my own would have taken me an additional ten years, had I not been able to rely on the advice and instruction of friends and family members, like Lamar Sanders and his father, Cecil, to help me unravel some of the mysteries that lay at my feet in the sand ruts of the St. Regis grade.

The advice given plus being taught proper use of turkey calls of all types by men who were masters of the art, made the transition from novice to turkey hunter a very swift and pleasant rite of passage.

I was taught the use of the call now referred to as a scratch box, which is a small cedar box call and cedar or slate striker, by Richard Wallace of Williston, Florida. Richard handmade this type of yelper and was a true master in its use. In his hands it could be made to bring forth clucks, purrs, and any number of soft or loud yelps, with never a mistake. He made and gave me the finest call of this type I have ever used or seen, and with Richard as my teacher I learned and did very well with this call in a short period of time.

The stories he told me of hunts that took place in years past and also some of his hunts in the mid-fifties fired me up to become a better hunter. He was always pleased to answer any questions that I asked. I gained a great deal of knowledge from this kind and good man and I enjoyed the hours spent in his company.

When I married my companion of thirty-nine years, it was not with turkey hunting in mind but in marrying this lady, I received a package deal worth a lot to a fellow who wanted to become a good turkey hunter. Almost all of the uncles and cousins on her mother's side of the family were the grandest bunch of woodsmen and hunters to be found anywhere and all could read signs made in game trails and on sand roads, and understood what they saw there as well as a Harvard lawyer can read a law book.

All were helpful to me in every way. Cecil Sanders and his son, Lamar, became my mentors and I do believe that without the help that each one of them gave me, I would know a lot less than I do today about the wild turkey and its hunting.

No man ever had better hunting companions or better teachers. Lamar's young brother Roy was just a seven-year-old boy at the time but he would arrive at our trailer at 8:00 A.M. to guide my wife on squirrel hunts. This of course freed me to search for turkeys. They always did well on these hunts. Roy is grown now and a good woodsman in his own right. I am indebted to Sam Poore, my uncle by marriage, for teaching me the use of the wing bone. Once again as in the use of the box call, I was taught by a master. Sam could make a turkey take notice, and any other turkey hunter in the area also. His calls would compete with any hen alive. Frank Schilling, my old friend and mentor, gave and taught me to use my first slate and peg call. I would take it to Iller's poultry market in St. Petersburg, Florida and listen to the turkeys that Mr. Iller had in crates in the back of the store awaiting their fate. I would yelp and cluck, and they in turn would answer me. It was a beginning.

When I look at all of the VCR and cassette tapes that are available today to teach the beginning turkey hunter what a turkey sounds like in the wild, I am astonished. I think of the series of cassette tapes titled *Real Turkeys.* This series of four tapes were made at Fish Eating Creek, in Florida by Dr. Lovett Williams and David Austin. At the time both men were employed by the Florida Game and Fresh Water Fish Commission while doing a study of the wild turkey that took the greater part of twenty years.

In these tapes, Dr. Williams gives a running narrative describing the type of call that each turkey is making and the reason it is giving this call. He also states whether it is a hen or a gobbler calling. This is a most informative set of tapes. One you can run and rerun, learning something each time, while rehearsing your calling until you and your diaphragm sound just like the turkey doing the calling on the tape.

Dr. Williams has written a number of books related to the life cycle and also hunting of the wild turkey. Along with the books he has written, he has brought back the wonderful old classic *The American Wild Turkey* by Henry E. Davis along with two other books that have been out of print since the 1920s. Lovett deserves a large pat on the back for bringing these three books back for the public to enjoy and learn from.

I would like to say at this point that perhaps the greatest aid made available at this date to the beginning hunter is the VCR. This is the magic carpet that can place anyone, expert or novice, right in the blind with some of the state and world championship callers, showing one and all at close range just how the cow ate the cabbage. No matter what the stage your experience is in, you will pick up something from the tape "The Truth about Spring Gobbler Hunting" by Will Primos and Friends, and if you can't learn something from Danny Kretzer's calling on Donny Kerby's tape *Spring Fever* then you are not looking or listening hard enough.

Ray Eye can also teach the man who wants to learn a thing or two about calling turkeys, the proper use of the mouth call, scouting the area, reading sign, knowing what to look for, and how to set up your gobbler after you have found him. All of this is on the VHS tape "Eye of the Turkey" Part I and Part II. The working of the last turkey that is killed on "Eye On the Turkey Number One," had some of the best diaphragm calling you will ever hear.

Not many men can drop from a flat out excited series of cutting to almost a half speed, low volume then a mid-range series of yelps. This has to be seen and heard to appreciate. Beginning hunters never had it so good. I have only one thing to say to today's beginning turkey hunter. Don't let anyone tell you about the good old days being gone. The good old days are here and now. Turkey restoration by game departments throughout the states have given all but a few states a huntable population of turkeys. Four-by-four vehicles will tackle the worse swamp and get you where you need to go, and VCR movies can teach you in a short time everything that would have taken you years to learn on your own in years past.

A new breed of shotguns, some that throw a ninety-two percent load of numbers fours at forty yards into a thirty-inch circle. Who could ask for more? There are a few flies in our turkey ointment. However, we have a number of people in the country today that believe it is morally wrong to hunt any animal or bird, for whatever reason, with anything but a camera. A lot of these folks eat meat and enjoy it greatly, but they are strongly adverse to taking the life of a game bird or animal. Some of them may be won over given time, honest answers to their questions, and if possible an explanation of why we who love to hunt, do this thing, if we ourselves can fully understand it and the full intensity of this obsession. Most of us who have hunted from childhood and on into what is commonly called old age.

I am sure that the people who feel such a strong aversion to hunting do so because they have never been exposed to the real side of nature. They, never having been there, cannot understand what it is like to be twenty miles from the nearest human being, sitting quietly, waiting in a blind that you have built, in which you will wait for a band of six old gobblers to come by because the sign that you have read in the sand in front of your blind has told you that they were there yesterday, and if a wild cat or fox or even a rambling urge that makes them want to see the other side of the creek doesn't beset them, they should return today.

Your vigil may be a long one, perhaps daylight to dark without the sight of the six long beards that you came there to observe. But the day was not lost, not by a long shot; first the owls hooting and laughing, then the sounds of the whole forest waking up with bird calls of all kinds followed by red birds and brown thrashers feeding and playing around your blind, then the sunlight falling on a spider web covered with dew and each droplet hanging there reflects every color of the spectrum caused by the undulation each time a breeze touches the edge of the web. There is also the pleasant sound of the drumming away of a woodpecker off in the distance, then the wild and mad sound of the pileated woodpecker calling in flight. You notice columns of ants working from the ground up the tree side by your blind in a never-ending stream, busy, busy, ever busy; and now a flight of wood ducks leaving the cypress pond and a gray fox trots by, stops, sniffs about, and trots on. A deer is seen, then another and another until there they stand, the whole family, the old doe and her two half-grown yearlings, and so it goes.

This is the part the anti- and no-hunter never gets to see. They have been led to believe that all hunters have only one interest and that is the killing of game. I am sure that most of you who have hunted for more than twenty years will concede that the hunt just described on the past few pages would be judged by you as being a very satisfying and fulfilling experience although no gun was fired and no game killed. This is not to say that this man will quit hunting, it's just that now he will kill less. He will still provide a turkey for the Thanksgiving Day table, and if he is a deer hunter you can bet his freezer will have enough venison to feed eight people at one setting. I am only trying to say that this man will derive almost as much pleasure from watching and calling turkeys as he once did from shooting them.

I will say here that we have our hands full now with the ever-increasing antigun and anti-hunting factions. The line is drawn and the opposition has amassed a great deal of money and has the names and support of some of the most prestigious people in the show business industry. We at this point cannot afford to falter or lag behind in our support of those who are fighting for our rights to own firearms and for our rights to take our guns to the woods and fields for a day of recreation. Those of us who enjoy hunting will have to fight a continuous battle now and in years to come. We have shifted from the time our country was rural, or rather it was urban at the time we entered into World War II, to one that has become very close to being populated by city dwellers and with this comes the urbanized way of thinking about the world at large.

Our children are taught in the classroom by teachers who were watching *Bambi* when they were children growing up, and who would not say that fuzzy animals that talk and act like human beings are not beguiling. Many children of the sixties are strict vegetarians who eat no meat of any kind, see the killing of any game animal or slaughter of even livestock as cruel and inhumane. They also see the wearing of furs or any form of animal skin, even leather, as being as sinful as the breaking of one of the Ten Commandments.

In all of the stories or documentaries that I have seen on television, I have yet to see a hunter depicted as a naturalist or a nature lover. Any form of hunting seen on television seems to show the man holding the gun as a person who is unwashed, unshaven, unclean, and unsavory in every respect, unable to speak an intelligent word, only able to articulate at a third-grade level, and he mumbles at that. This man presents the perfect image of the term in use by the children of today when they say "gross." Is it any wonder that with all of the antihunting and antigun images being fed by the media to the kids of today that they could take a kindly view of the hunter when they never get to see a real one in the real world?

I might inject here that it does not help our public image when we wear tee shirts stating "Happiness is a large gut pile," and "Patience hell, I want to kill something." This type of thing, if it must be worn at all, is better worn in camp than in public. We have reached a point that we must have a better image if we are to survive.

Become active in your local and state conservation movements and if you can afford to, join, and I honestly don't see how those of us who hunt can afford not too. The wildlife legislative fund of America, United Conservation Alliance, and the N.R.A. all have men who are dedicated, intelligent, articulate spokesmen who can carry the debate to whatever part of the arena it is needed. Write and call your congressman to tell him what you think of the bills being drafted that can affect your sport, and ask him how he intends to vote on the bills that will affect your recreation, perhaps for the rest of your life. I would add that everyone likes a pat on the back and your representatives and senators need this when they fight in our behalf. Don't write just to complain.

As I penned the last line the phone rang and I found I was speaking to my good friend Lentho Burns, the retired conservation officer from the state of New Jersey, and a discussion took place regarding the various antihunting groups at work in the halls of legislature today. In the course of this conversation, Lentho told me of a situation that had occurred in townships of Hopewell and Princeton in the state of New Jersey. Both townships in the 1970s had become quite heavily populated. A large amount of acreage in both townships contained estates that were valued in excess of a million dollars and while not every person in this area was living on a million-dollar estate, many who lived there were affluent. As this section began to grow the residents of both townships began to petition the New Jersey Game and Fish Commission to close both townships to deer hunting, and they were successful. I am sure that all who read this know what happened in a relatively short period of time. Game commissioners and the biologists who make the study of animals their life work have given us figures that state that a pair of deer in a protected environment can within ten years produce a herd of 150 deer, if successful in breeding each year and then if each of the prodigy produced by this breeding is as successful in their breeding as the parents. Let us compound the problem by saying we have a 150 deer to the area to start with and then allow no form of hunting to take place. As I understand it from the story told to me by Lentho Burns, this was the point the two townships arrived at in less than ten years.

The deer herd was out of control. The food normally browsed on was almost gone, the deer were destroying fruit orchards. No one could grow a garden in the area. Mighty raids were made on front lawns where any form of hedge, flower, grapevine, costly ornamental fruit tree, or even potted plants sitting on the steps were eaten. In short the deer had begun the slow process of starvation. The same people who had fought with the game department about closing both townships to hunting were now clambering to have someone, anyone, come in and reduce the size of this silent herd that came each night to eat almost anything it found growing.

Public meetings were held and it was finally decided that an open season using hunters might prove to be dangerous due to the growth that had taken place in both areas. When the voting was over the job of removing a large number of deer in each township fell on the shoulders of a few handpicked officers within the game department.

Officer Burns was told to reduce the deer herd in his area in short order and I believe that the department wanted him to remove somewhere close to sixty deer from his area. He owned and was using as his personal deer rifle, a Winchester model 70 in cal. 30-06. He was uncomfortable with the thought of using a rifle with that much power in a congested area. Officer Burns drove to the custom gun shop of Gus Shelke, a man renowned for his fine custom-built rifles at that period of time. He discussed his dilemma with Mr. Shelke and in a few seconds, Mr. Shelke came from the back of the shop with the answer to the problem. He handed Lentho a lightweight 243 that he had built for himself and three boxes of 100 grain hand-loaded ammunition. If I remember correctly this lightweight rifle had a three-power post and cross hair receptacle. Lentho Burns, not a man to brag but yet known in his department as a fine rifle shot, told me that he removed eighty-two deer in about thirty days. He stated that distance seemed to make little difference to this rifle. Many of his shots were made at 200 yards and a few at close to 500. The really long shots of course were made with the aid of a jacket rolled up and put on the hood of his patrol car to obtain a rock steady rest to shoot from. All in all they killed 800 deer in the combined townships.

The point of the story just told is one that biologist and game commissions throughout the United States are very familiar with and due to politics must deal with from time to time. The results are always the same. You can not stockpile wildlife. Overprotected herds of deer will soon be on a collision course with land owners and starvation if not kept in check.

Turkeys fair no better when they are too numerous for the area they must range in. Fowl pox, black head, and other diseases of the intestinal tract are waiting around the corner to wipe out many whole flocks at a time. It is in our best interest to support the programs developed by the game departments of the states we live in. The men in charge of the various programs of game and fish in your state have more than likely devoted most of their adult life in both the classroom and in the field to maintain and also increase, where possible, the game and fish populations in your area. Help them in every way you can for in working with them and giving them your full support, you will be providing yourself with better hunting and fishing.

As we near the end of this book, I would like to touch on several things that I feel I should address before bringing it to an end. I have mixed feelings about the subject I want to talk about now.

It is the use of hen decoys in the spring gobbling season. I have used hen decoys for the past four seasons and have killed three big gobblers while using them and pulled up another really big gobbler that turned and walked away because he did not care for the cold-acting lady that stood there and would not move after calling to him for ten minutes. Even though it is legal I still feel that I am cheating. I don't know why this feeling should persist but it does. I feel somehow that I am taking an unfair advantage of the bird when I work him with a hen decoy. I have discussed this with friends and they ask, "How many ducks have you called and killed over decoys? Did you feel bad about this? Well, then don't feel bad about using Heney Penny or Peggy Sue to help bring the big man in, because it is your calling that is the real veil of illusion, you are a real decoy." Yet when I look out twenty-five yards from my blind and there she stands, looking so damn real, I have a strange feeling. Perhaps I will overcome this feeling in time and will then fully enjoy the bird I did not intend to shoot, and I have always known what type of bird or animal I have been shooting at the time I shot it and its sex. I have never had a hunting accident or even a close call. I am a lover of the lightweight rifle and have owned some good ones in .22 Hornet, .222 Remington, .218 M. Bee. I have killed a lot of turkeys with the .222 Remington, and the 218 Mashburn Bee with both cartridges loaded down to .22 Hornet velocities.

I have killed many more turkeys at forty yards with a rifle than I have at ranges beyond forty. I am a lover of good side-by-side double-barrel shotguns and also over-and unders, and if I could only have one gun to hunt turkeys with it would not be the rifle, it would be the shotgun. If the range is right and the charge is right, the shotgun is certain, every time. The man with the shotgun can be shaking like a leaf, moving the barrels in short jerks and circles, but at the last moment, when he slaps the trigger, the turkey will still be shot and killed, if in range. This will not take place with the rifle. The shot will have to be controlled, with no barrel movement, and the trigger squeezed slowly, not slapped or there will be no turkey at your feet. It will have flown away. So why do I still use the rifle from time to time? Don't ask me, as I cannot tell you. I guess the closest answer would be because I like the idea of being able to take a 100-yard shot if I have to. I have missed a lot of those 100-yard shots over the years though. So perhaps I use the rifle from time to time as a conservation measure.

As I have said before, when you turn loose a one-and-five-eighths-ounce-load of copper-plated number fives on a turkey within a proper range, you are going to take him home with you. You can't make that statement about the rifle. I guess that most of us who have hunted turkeys for a number of years have had the unsettling experience of calling up another hunter within eyesight of our blind.

Most of the time when this occurs, we know we are yelping to a hunter and not a turkey. I have found over the past few years that I am not always sure if it is a turkey answering my calling or another hunter.

We have a new breed of turkey hunters with us today. They may be short on experience, as only years can give them this, but they have paid their dues when it comes to watching videotapes and listening to Lovette Williams' *Real Turkeys* tapes, I through IV, or any one of a dozen other good cassette tapes that teach the calls of the wild turkey. They have also bought and learned how to use two or three good yelpers.

These fellows will bring you back to life after that last cup of coffee has played out. I have had some of these chaps raise the hair on the back of my neck when I was just about to let my chin hit my chest. Be careful, boys, because this is the way it comes about. These fellows will be in shooting distance of your blind before you know it. If you check game commission accidents records over the past twenty years, you will find many statements that run something to this effect: Hunter was in a blind and was mistaken for a turkey as he was eating an apple; the shooter was thirty-five yards away when he shot at what he thought was the movement of a real turkey and inside the blind, the victim was hit on the right side of his face, neck, shoulder, and hand with a short mag twelve-gauge load of number fives; not fatal.

I want to state here and now that our sport is only as safe as we choose to make it. Unless we take certain precautions when we hunt turkey from a blind and with a call, no one of us is beyond the possibility of being shot. Russ Smiley, the renowned Florida wildlife watercolor artist and long-time, avid turkey hunter was shot a few years back.

A friend, who shall remain nameless here, was with my son and I when my son killed his first turkey in a dried up cypress swamp at Interlachen, Florida many years ago. This man was shot after calling a young boy up twice in one day. He had told the boy never to try to sneak up on a flock of turkeys because it was very hard to do. Instead, he should get a yelper and learn how to call, then build a blind and call the turkey to you. My friend called this young chap up again that afternoon and the young man shot him in the back as he called from within his blind. This man's wife was shot two years later while yelping to a turkey; both are old-time native Floridians who have hunted all of their lives and were close to the half-century mark in age when both shootings occurred. If what I have just written has had a sobering influence on your thoughts about turkey hunting that is good, for this is the reason it was written.

How do we go about keeping ourselves intact and yet enjoy our sport? Well, a number of people I know have approached it in different moves. Tom Gaskins once told me that he had used a white muslin banner with large red letters that read turkey hunter inside. He wrapped this banner above his blind. He stated the turkeys didn't mind the banner and no one shot him while he used it. He thought perhaps it was effective. I know of other hunters placing several rounds of surveyors' fluorescent tape around trees above their blind. In recent years I use die cut two-color camo (fall and spring) on the other ten-foot long by fifty-two-inch high with three iron stakes. I find a very large tree that will cover my back completely and one in which my forward view will cover 180 degree left to right. I set up so that hardly anyone can come up behind me or to my sides without being seen.

I use palmetto fronds, broom sedge, dog fennels, Spanish moss, and bits of oak and other trees to help blend in. It looks good, is almost invisible, and the best part is that it is ninety-nine percent safe. The other one percent is up to me. If I feel that something is playing games or calling to me thinking I am a turkey and this feeling persists for any length of time, I have a sure fire thing that ends a calling contest with another hunter. I just start whistling Dixie over and over two or three times. Most of the good ole boys will leave the area on hearing this. If, however, you really have been working with a turkey, have no fear, southern turkeys are right at home with a proper rendition of Dixie, and if you have not stood up and given a rebel yell or exposed yourself above your blind, a little more yelping tacked on to the end of this fine old tune will bring a turkey to your blind just as though nothing had happened. If you use a decoy you must be especially careful in its placement. Never have a decoy in the road where a hunter coming from the opposite side of your decoy could shoot at the decoy and at the same time put his shot charge into your blind. Always have your decoy blocked from the back side by a large tree, dense thicket or cypress pond, so that any shooting that might be done at the decoy would be done at an angle away from your blind. It really only takes a little common sense to be safe. Just remember the better you are in using your calls, the more natural you will sound, thus the more careful you must be in observing the area around you for other hunters.

I recall the only time I was ever really frightened, I was hunting the St. Regis management area in Dixie County, in a place called Garnto Hammock. I arrived at this lovely hourglass-shaped hammock at midafternoon and after scouting the outside edge of the hammock, I looked at my watch and found that it was 3:15 P.M. The sign that I had seen in the sandy flat that lay at the entrance of the first hammock had quickened my pulse for there was an abundance of turkey sign made just a short time before I had arrived and the line of march was all in a westerly direction along the trail that led into the first hammock. I eased on along the trail until I came to the entrance to the first hammock. I slipped on inside and looked around in the sandy opening at the front of the southern part of Garnto Hammock. It was covered with turkey sign and all of it smoking hot. I eased over to one side and sat down in a newly cut fire line. I quickly cut a double handful of palmetto fronds and gathered some moss and dog fennels and within five minutes I had a very respectable blind.

I sat in it for two hours, yelping and clucking at intervals. I received no answer for my effort. About five P.M. I got up and waded the small creek that ran between the two hammocks that were called by the same name. I came out of the creek into Garnto Hammock west (my name for it, the folks who lived there called them both just Garnto Hammock). I stood and looked from behind each tree as I eased along searching for this flock that I believed to be, unless I had misread the sign, somewhere very close to me in the second hammock. I could see or hear no sound of turkeys feeding and I felt I should have. I made a quick blind, I sat down, pulled out my slate and peg, and began to do a bit of contented purring and pit-pit-piting, followed by low yelps, very low. I received an answer and I in turn answered back. This bird clucked to me and I would purr and cluck back. A minute would pass and then I would get three or four yelps and not very good ones. I would answer in kind. A minute or two would pass and this bird would yelp five or six times.

It was getting late now. I clucked and yelped three or four times. The answer came back quickly but it was ragged, something was just not right. The tone was off-key and by now the turkey should have stepped out in the open as it would soon be flying up time. Five minutes passed and then I started giving a very rapid series of pit-pit calls, the type often given by an old hen just before flying up. I followed this with a six- or seven-note yelp. At this point I began to have the strangest feeling that there was another hunter stalking me and that he was very close by.

I have read that just before lightning strikes, people have stated the hair on their head and neck gave the sensation of standing up and this was very close to the feeling I experienced. Late that afternoon in Garnto Hammock, in the last moments, I felt sure I was about to be shot, I threw myself on the ground at the same time yelling, "Don't shoot!" I laid there prone for a minute or two and when I stood up the feeling was gone and whatever I had been yelping to was gone also.

I tried to find fresh tracks in the area that the yelping was coming from but could find none, manmade, turkey or otherwise. I have yelped up other hunters before this happening and some since, but never before have I felt that I was in any danger of being shot except on this occasion. It was a strange feeling but I have come to believe that it was after all, a lone turkey. Given a few more minutes I would have more than likely heard this turkey fly up to roost. I feel sure that my shouting ran it out of the hammock. It was a very quiet evening and if this bird or any of the flock that had made the fresh sign at the entrance and along the trail leading into Garnto Hammock had flown up anywhere in either one of the hammocks, I should have heard them go up. I feel that this flock went out through the north end of the second hammock to roost over the little creek that runs through the area, using the roosting site where this flock felt most secure.

I wonder how many of you reading this have lost a turkey due to some small mistake that you made in working the bird and perhaps, lost him that last sixty yards, when you thought everything was going just right. Well, don't call for the crying towel just yet or feel too badly because it comes to us all, and if we hunt a long season, spring and fall, it may happen to us once or twice each season.

I have just received a phone call from and old and valued friend this morning. Our relationship runs back thirty years and a little more, to a time when we were both employees of the Florida Game and Fresh Water Fish Commission. It has been a pleasant friendship in every way. Jamie Adams and this is the person I write of has the gift of making everyone around them feel at ease. I first became aware of this after teaching a number of black powder classes to the students at Sumter High School. I was a firearms safety instructor as well as a pilot for the commission at this time. This was a very pleasant time in my life, as I always enjoyed teaching the classes on the safe use and fun of muzzle loading, shooting, and hunting. A short time after I began teaching the courses at the high school, Jamie and I were requested to attend the commission supervisor's school in Tallahassee Florida. It was at this time that I began to realize that there were many facets that formed this fellow's makeup. He is a fine woodsman, hunter, tracker, and public speaker, and his love of the wild turkey, as the good book says, surpasses all understanding.

I will state here that in most communities, there is always a handful of men who study and read every wild turkey video and magazine that is available, and there are many excellent ones to be had. The Will Primos series "The Truth about Turkey Hunting" is an excellent start. They buy new calls each season (with a gun cabinet full of every type of call ever made and to compound matters, these guys will call endlessly). Most of their calls are done once or twice a week and at all hours of the day and night until the lady of the house swears that if she hears one more cluck, yelp or cackle, she will move out. If you are a dyed-in-the-wool turkey hunter you know whereof I speak. Jamie fits this pattern perfectly. I might also add that you may tar me with the same brush.

A few years passed after I had taught muzzle-loading classes at Bushnell. I began to hear people say that Jamie would make a good sheriff and that he should throw his hat in the ring. He did and as the saying goes the rest is history. He was the high sheriff of Sumter County for sixteen years and had a fine administration, with nothing but praise from the people of Sumter County and other surrounding counties.

It was during this period of time that Jamie fell totally in love with the wild turkey and was able to devote some of his time to building a conservation foundation among the hunters, bird watchers, and nature lovers in Sumter County and in the areas around it. He did this by reading every worthwhile paper and book written from creditable writers and biologists. He had the woodsmanship already. He went on to become the president of the Sumter County chapter of the National Wild Turkey Federation, and his yearly banquets, calling contests, and auctions of paintings, calls, and many other types of hunting equipment always played to a full house. The food was consistently fine and there was lots of it. I have attended many banquets given by Jamie that reached an almost standing-room-only turnout. A short time after his retirement as sheriff of Sumter County, Jamie was asked to join ranks as a field representative for one of the most prestigious call companies and video film producers in the country. I speak of Will Primos Game Calls. This firm makes almost every type of turkey call known to man and believe me, they know how to do it. Their quality control is second to none.

The true double-diaphragm call made in their workshop is one of the deadliest calls I have ever used. The series of video movies *The Truth About Turkey Hunting* is one of the most informative methods of teaching a young man the art of calling and hunting turkeys that I have ever seen and now there is even a tape for young kids.

Good things unlike trouble do not usually come in bunches but shortly after becoming a representative for Primos, Jamie was appointed to the board of directors of the Game and Fresh Water Fish Commission, in the state of Florida. In receiving the honor of this appointment the hunters, bird watchers, fishermen, and lovers of nature have reaped a bounty that will just get better as time goes by. For in placing this man on the board, the public will have the ear of a man who has done it all and will listen, fairly evaluate, and act on any proposals concerning the game, fish and habitat of the state. I reiterate, he will be fair. If you have a fellow in your state who works as hard to increase the turkey population, give him a hand. Attend the yearly N.W.T.F. banquet and auctions and join the National Wild Turkey Federation Organizations. Work every day of the year in one of these organizations, and the turkey hunter will not face a bleak future.

Last Page

I recall sitting on an old-time front porch on a rainy afternoon, with Lovett Williams and we were indulging in a short libation, discussing life in general. In short, we were enjoying a grand time as I recall it. We had just filled our glasses when I asked Lovett why a man, who had the reputation of being the best turkey hunter in a certain county, would resort to using corn to bait turkeys. I told him that another wildlife officer and I had sat in a spot for three days over a pile of corn a show dog could not jump over. We sat there, but our man never showed and I really believed that we were both glad that he did not. The man who had put the corn out was eighty years old, a pillar of society in the community he lived in, and a deacon in the First Baptist Church of the main city in the county and was known for his kindness and honesty to one and all. I told Lovett that I could not understand the reason that this man above all men would resort to baiting to kill a turkey. Lovett gave me that little grin that he has and said, "Phil, this is an easy one to explain. The old fellow has had the prestige of basking in the limelight of being the best turkey hunter in this part of the state for fifty years and some folks might say that hailed from this section of Florida, that they would rather have his reputation than be governor of the state, but as in all things Father Time begins to catch up with all of us. The creeks he could once wade up to his shirt pocket in seem to have gotten deeper, the water colder, and crossing fences, legal or illegal, are harder to get over. A three-mile walk to a favorite hammock that seemed to be no more than stepping out in the yard to pick up the morning paper now makes every muscle, knee, and hip joint feel like a sore tooth. Why, Phil, you can understand that. This fellow now had to resort to flocks of birds that are closer to town where he can drive to set out his little piles of bait. With this he can still kill a few birds each year and still be able to maintain his reputation. Lovett looked at me and winked as he took another sip. He said "Phil, come to think of it, you are getting about that age too."

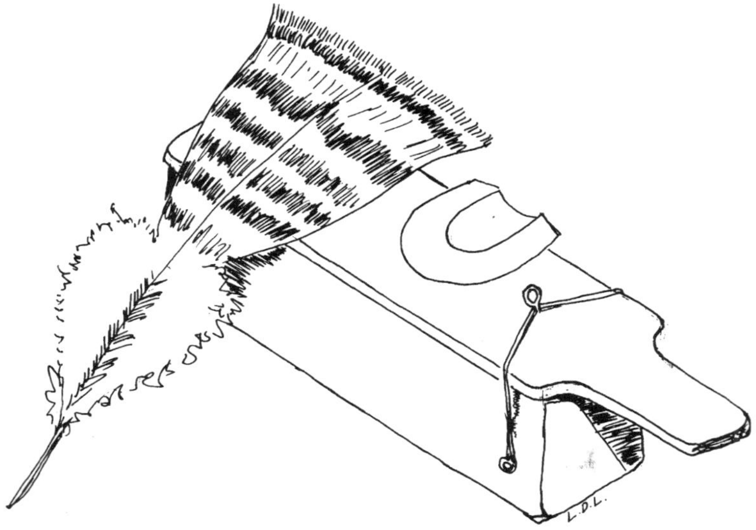

Turkey Call Box